Edward Jo...

SPIRIT
of the GAME

GOAL LINE STAND
BOOK 1

BY TODD HAFER

Zonderkidz

This book is dedicated to the life and memory
of Tim Hanson, a true athlete, a true friend.

Zonder**kidz**.

The children's group of Zondervan

www.zonderkidz.com

Goal Line Stand
Copyright © 2004 by Todd Hafer

Requests for information should be addressed to:
Zonderkidz, Grand Rapids, Michigan 49530

Library of Congress Cataloging-in-Publication Data

Hafer, Todd.
  Goal line stand / by Todd Hafer.
    p. cm.–(The spirit of the game, sports fiction series)
  Summary: After his mother dies, thirteen-year-old Cody has trouble
concentrating on football and faces some challenges in his relationships with
teammates.
    ISBN 0-310-70669-6 (softcover)
    [1. Christian life—Fiction. 2. Football—Fiction. 3. Friendship—Fiction.]
I. Title.
    PZ7.H11975Go 2004
    [Fic]—dc22
                                                    2004012893

Editor: Bruce Nuffer
Cover design by Alan Close
Interior design: Susan Ambs
Art direction: Laura Maitner
Photos by Synergy Photographic
Printed in the United States of America

04 05 06 07 08/❖DC/5 4 3 2 1

Contents

Foreword

I love sports. I have always loved sports. I have competed in various sports at various levels, right through college. And today, even though my official competitive days are behind me, you can still find me on the golf course, working on my game, or on a basketball court, playing a game of pick-up.

Sports have also helped me learn some of life's important lessons–lessons about humility, risk, dedication, teamwork, friendship. Cody Martin, the central character in "The Spirit of the Game" series, learns these lessons too. Some of them, the hard way. I think you'll enjoy following Cody in his athletic endeavors.

Like most of us, he doesn't win every game or every race. He's not the best athlete in his school, not by a long shot. But he does taste victory, because, as you'll see, he comes to understand that life's greatest victories aren't reflected on a scoreboard. They are the times when you rely on a strength beyond your own —a spiritual strength—to carry you through. They are the times when you put the needs of someone else before your own. They are the times when sports become a way to celebrate the life God has given you.

So read on, and may you always possess the true spirit of the game.

Toby McKeehan

The Battle Begins

Cody Martin prowled the chewed-up turf behind the Raider defensive line, eyes surveying the scene in front of him. His teammates on the D-line were hunkered down in their three-point stances, like attack dogs ready to be unleashed, anchored by Pork Chop at middle guard. Cody noticed a deep bruise the size of a beverage coaster in the middle of his best friend's bulging, caramel-skinned calf.

"Motion left! Monster left!" Cody barked, his voice ragged and hoarse after three and a half quarters of calling defensive signals. He studied Rick Macy, Central Middle School's fleet wideout, as he trotted parallel to the line of scrimmage.

"Motion man's mine!" Cody called, whipping his head around to make eye contact with Brett Evans, Grant Middle School's left cornerback. "You got eighty-two, Brett!"

Brett nodded.

Cody shadowed Macy as Antwan Clay, the Grizzly quarterback, called out his snap count. On Clay's third "Hut!" Macy turned upfield as the Central and Grant lines surged forward, and Cody heard the familiar crack of pads fill the late-afternoon air. While the two lines battled each other for a few feet of turf, Clay faked a handoff to his halfback, tucked the ball in the crook of his arm, and sprinted toward Cody.

A QB sweep, Cody thought. *So that's why they brought two wideouts to the same side.*

Macy was on Cody now, trying to bulldoze him out of bounds. That meant Clay was going to cut inside. Cody raised his hands in front of him and chucked Macy sharply across the chest. Macy's body straightened, as if he had been hit by a strong headwind.

That was all the opportunity Cody needed. He slipped inside his taller opponent and zeroed in on Clay as the QB planted his right foot and made his cut upfield.

You're mine, Cody thought, as he lunged for Clay's legs.

Cody never saw Tucker, Central's huge fullback, coming up on his right flank. But he felt him. One moment he was flying toward his target—the next, his flight was abruptly redirected.

At first there was no pain, only the resounding bang of Tucker's face mask against the side of Cody's helmet. Crumpled on the turf, Cody listened for the shrill ripple of a referee's whistle. But there was no sound.

Well, either Clay is well on his way to the end zone or that hit rendered me deaf, he thought.

He tried to sit up but felt a sharp dagger of pain between his neck and right shoulder. *Please, God,* he prayed silently, desperately, *don't let me get injured during the first game of the season. I need football right now, more than ever. Please!*

Cody tried to smile as the blond kid with a head like a lunchbox kneeled over him. "Hey, Dutch," Cody said weakly.

"Hey, Code," the team trainer answered. "Just lie still. Coach Smith is on his way."

On cue, Coach Smith appeared at Dutch's side. "Mean hit you took," he observed. "That's why I'm always tellin' you, don't leave your feet on a tackle. So, Martin, did you just get your bell rung or are you hurt?"

"Huh?" Cody said, blinking his eyes.

"Hurt," Coach Smith said, impatience creeping into his voice. "You know, pain. Are you in pain?"

Am I in pain? Cody thought. *What a question! I've been in pain for almost two months straight. You think football is tough, Coach? Try watching your mom die.*

Chapter 1

A Death in the Family

As Cody lay on the field, his mind drifted back to the day of his mom's funeral.

Cody squirmed in the front pew of Crossroads Community Church, trying to wriggle his way into a comfortable position. He sighed heavily and twisted around to study the scene behind him. He felt dozens of eyes lock on him, then nervously dart away. Except for those of Mrs. Adams, his grade school Sunday school teacher, who gazed at him lovingly. She was five rows back, but Cody could see that her eyes were red and puffy from crying. He tried to smile at her and then turned around. He usually sat in the back of church—the very back, in one of the metal folding chairs lined against the rear wall of the sanctuary.

"The best seats in the house," Cody always called them. They allowed him to slip out to the restroom or the foyer without disapproving stares from his mom and dad—or that busybody Mrs. Underwood. And, during the occasional Sunday when he couldn't follow Pastor Taylor's sermon, he could pass the time by counting bald spots, then figuring the percentage of follically-impaired men in the congregation. The last time he counted, 23 percent of the Crossroads men were Missing Hair Club candidates.

The percentage was slightly higher if you counted Mr. Sanders, whose sandy toupee always rested atop his head at a jaunty angle, like a dozing badger.

On the rare Sundays when Pork Chop accompanied Cody to church, the duo would slip out to the foyer during the special music—which usually wasn't very special at Crossroads—and feast on the remaining donuts on the refreshment table.

The good donuts, the ones filled with jelly or crowned with multi-colored sprinkles, were always gone, plucked by those devoted enough to come to the early service. But the remainder, the glazed ones with watery icing beading on them like perspiration, were better than nothing.

"Donuts—at church!?" Chop said once while sucking glaze off his fingers with loud smacks. "Now that's a heavenly idea! It's almost worth coming to church every Sunday. Almost."

Cody leaned forward and rested his elbows on his knees. Pork Chop was in church again today, but there would be no joking. Chop sat three rows behind Cody, sporting a too tight suit and sandwiched between his father and his mammoth half brother, Doug.

Cody had begged his dad to let Pork Chop sit by him, but had been informed that such an arrangement wasn't "proper funeral protocol."

Cody was bookended by his dad and Gram Martin, his paternal grandmother. Cody looked at Gram, who looked older, plumper, and sadder than the last time he saw her, even though it was just two weeks ago. She was sniffling quietly and dabbing at her eyes with a tattered lavender tissue. It was no secret that Cody's mom and Gram Martin didn't get along, but the grief seemed genuine.

Or maybe it's regret, Cody thought. Maybe Gram is thinking of all the shouting matches she and Mom got into and feeling guilty.

He turned his attention from his grandmother to the coffin at the front of the church, just below the pulpit.

I can't believe my mom's in there, he thought, shaking his head. But it was true. He saw her in there only twelve hours ago. He had waited patiently in the foyer, pawing at the carpet with his foot as he listened to the choir practice "Amazing Grace," which was his mom's favorite hymn during the final weeks of her life. The choir sounded somber, but pretty good—better than he had heard in a long time.

When the singing stopped, Ben Woods, of Woods Family Funeral Home, approached Cody. "You can see her now, if you wish," Ben said, with a calmness and compassion that Cody guessed had taken years to perfect.

Wish. The word floated through his mind. I wish this whole thing wasn't real, he thought. I wish I were anywhere but here. I wish Mom weren't lying dead in a giant box.

Cody felt Ben's fingers touch his elbow. "Would you like me to get your father, Cody, so you can go in together? He's in the pastor's office."

"No," Cody said, surprised at how hard it was to make a sound. "I kinda need to do this alone."

Ben nodded and led Cody to the front of the sanctuary. With practiced ease, he raised the top portion of a two-piece lid and locked it into position.

"I will give you as long as you need," he said. "I'll close the sanctuary door behind me when I exit, to give you some privacy. Just come and find me when you're ready. And, Cody, I am very sorry for your loss."

Cody felt his head nodding. He had waited until he heard the door latch click before he allowed himself to look at her.

They had done her hair. Wispy honey-colored bangs rested on her forehead, the ends nearly touching her thin eyebrows. Cody noted the thick makeup layered on her face, like frosting on a cake. It reminded him of the makeup the high school thespians wore for their spring musicals.

He heard himself exhale sadly. When she was alive, Linda Martin rarely wore makeup. She used to joke that she wanted people to see a few lines on her face. "Maybe then they'll let me teach adult Sunday school—not just work the nursery," she would say.

Cody's dad had a different take. "You don't need makeup, Lin," he told her regularly. "Why cover up perfection?"

But the folks at Woods Family Funeral Home had covered up plenty. Cody remembered relatives talking about funerals from time to time. He recalled snippets like, "He looked so natural," and "She looked so peaceful lying there in the coffin."

But his mom didn't look natural or at peace. She looked empty. He studied her face. Slowly, tentatively, he raised his left hand. It floated toward her, as if under a power not his own.

He let his fingertips rest for a moment on her cheek. The skin felt cool, lifeless. More like rubber than human flesh. He drew his hand back.

I hope I forget how that felt, *he thought.* That's not how I want to remember things.

"Bye, Mom," *he whispered.* "And thank you. Thank you for everything you did. The meals—the laundry—the help with homework. Coming to my games. I wish I had been more grateful. I'll try to say something about you tomorrow, but I'm not sure I can. If I can't, I hope you'll understand. And I hope that, somehow, you know that I'll always love you. Please, God, let there be some way for her to know that—and to know how much I miss her already."

He felt his throat tighten. He turned toward the exit, gazing at the stained glass windows as he walked down the rust-colored carpet that ran down the center of the sanctuary. The last window depicted a sunrise scene, with a white dove gliding across the morning sky. Inscribed above a golden rising sun were the words, I AM THE RESURRECTION AND THE LIFE.

Before he opened the door leading to the foyer, Cody let his eyes move from the words to the church's high ceiling. "Yeah," he whispered solemnly, hopefully. "The life."

Cody felt himself being led to the sideline, Brett Evans under his left arm, Pork Chop under his right. Both were five foot eight, two inches taller than he was, so his feet glided across the short-cropped grass as they left the field. It felt almost like walking on air. He looked into the stands and saw about half the home crowd standing, rendering a polite smattering of applause. He searched for his dad's face, but knew he wouldn't find it.

This is gonna be just like seventh grade ball, he thought. *He's gonna keep blowing off games 'til the season's over. Only now I won't have Mom in the stands. I could always count on her. Now I don't have anybody.*

Pork Chop helped Cody lower himself to the bench. "It was Tucker who ear-holed you, right, Code?" he asked.

"Either him or a Mack truck."

"Well, just watch what happens next. It's gonna be payback time next time we're on defense. I'm gonna hit him so hard that it'll knock the taste out of his mouth."

"Chop—"

"Don't argue with me, my brother. Just chill and watch the fun. We're losing by twenty anyway. I gotta do something to keep myself motivated."

Cody started to protest and then shrugged his shoulders, which brought the stabbing pain back again.

Coach Smith kept him out of the game's final four minutes, during which Clay scored again on the QB sweep. On that play, Pork Chop chased down Tucker from behind and rode him to the ground, even though it was obvious that he was a blocker, not the ball carrier. After the referee raised both hands to the sky, signaling the TD, Chop smacked his palms against the sides of his helmet, feigning anger at himself for being duped. Then he extended a thick forearm to Tucker and jerked him to his feet.

Tucker stood, wobbly and disoriented. It reminded Cody of the newborn scene in *Bambi*. The fullback got off the field just in time to avoid Central's receiving an offside penalty on the ensuing kickoff.

By the Monday morning following the Central game, the pain in Cody's neck had faded. The pain in his heart, however, still burned. He smiled anyway.

He smiled at Coach Smith, who saw him in the hallway at school and asked, "You doin' okay, Code?"

He smiled at Robyn Hart, his friend since fourth grade, when she told him, "Good game on Saturday."

And he smiled at Kris Knight, the new student that Principal Prentiss introduced him to in the school office before first hour.

This is weird, Cody thought. *You don't even have to be happy to smile. Just like you don't have to be mean to play football. You just have to act like it, and I guess no one knows the difference.*

"Mr. Knight," Mr. Prentiss was saying, "welcome to the eighth grade at Grant Middle School. This is Cody Martin. This is his second year as one of our orientation mentors. He will be accompanying you to most of your classes, as your schedules are almost identical. He will help you find your classrooms, the cafeteria, and whatnot."

"Yeah," Cody said, injecting artificial happiness into his voice, "we have great whatnot here at Grant."

Mr. Prentiss unleashed a laugh that was as fake as Mr. Sanders's toupee.

As they headed toward first-period PE, Cody tried to think of a conversation starter. "So," he said finally to his "mentee," as Mr. Prentiss called them, "you do any sports back at your old school?"

Knight had arms like broomsticks, and Cody noticed that his feet splayed out at 45-degree angles when he walked. It was as if his left foot and right foot disagreed on which direction their owner should be going. Still, you had to ask. Polite conversation— that's what Dad and Mr. Prentiss called it.

Knight cleared his throat. "Nah, I'm not really into sports. I mean, I like them and everything, but I have asthma. I played in the pep band, though. Clarinet."

Cody nodded. "That's cool." He saw Knight looking at his white football jersey, which bore a faded blue number 7. John Elway's number.

Cody heard the throat clear again. It sounded like a dirt bike engine revving. "You must play, huh, Cody?"

"Yeah, I can't remember a time when I wasn't play-ing something. T-ball. Y-league hoops. Pop Warner football. Age-group track meets. You name it."

"That's cool," Knight said, unconvincingly.

They entered the gym and sat together on the first row of wooden bleachers. Ten boys, divided into shirts and skins, were playing full-court basketball. Another seven or eight sat on the bleachers near Cody and Knight, awaiting their turn.

Coach Smith, who taught PE in addition to coaching football and wrestling, paced the sideline, wearing a pained expression on his face.

"Come on, ladies," he chided, his voice weary and sandpaper-rough from the past weekend's game, "this is physical education. So let's get physical. Sewing class is third hour. Porter, if Alston beats your entire team down the court for one more uncontested layup, you knuckleheads are doing push-ups until your arms fall off!"

"Who's Porter?" Knight whispered loudly. "Is he that big dude?"

"Yeah," Cody said with a laugh, "the one who's sweatin' so much he looks like he's been dipped in baby oil. That's Pork Chop."

"Pork Chop?"

"Yeah. See, when he was a baby and cutting teeth, his dad used to give him pork chop bones to gnaw on. Drove his mom crazy, from what I've heard. Anyway, that's where the nickname comes from. His real name's Deke."

"That's his real name? What's it short for?"

"It's short for nothing. Just Deke."

Knight nodded. "What should I call him?"

"Well, Chop always says, 'Call me anything—just don't call me late for dinner!'"

Knight laughed politely.

Cody leaned back, resting his elbows on the second tier of bleachers. "I probably should tell you one thing about Chop," he said. "You probably notice that he's got quite a tan."

Knight nodded again.

"Well, his dad's white. His mom was black. Still is, I guess. She bounced a couple years ago. See, we don't have a lot of, uh, African-Americans in this part of Colorado. It was hard for Chop's mom. It's been hard for him too. I've been with him when people have driven by and called him—well, you know. You should see his eyes when it happens. I mean, he's a tough guy, but when people say stuff like that, racial stuff—"

"People still do that? In Colorado?"

"People still do that. And worse. Anyway, he can be a bit sensitive about the subject. Just so you know. But don't get the wrong idea. He's cool. He has a great sense of humor. Funniest guy in the school, as far as I'm concerned."

"So, you guys are friends?"

"Best friends." Cody felt his voice cracking as he said the words. He hoped Kris Knight didn't notice.

They turned their attention back to the game. They watched Pork Chop grab a rebound, swinging his elbows viciously from side to side as two opposing players tried to steal the ball from him. "Get offa me!" he snarled.

"Watch the 'bows, Chop," Coach Smith snapped.

"Wow," Knight said. "I wouldn't want Pork Chop mad at me."

Cody whistled through his teeth. "No," he said, "you sure wouldn't."

After one of Pork Chop's teammates shot an air ball from the free throw line, the shirts team gained control of the ball and launched a fast break. Their point guard drove down the middle of the court, stopped abruptly at the top of the key, and lofted a jump shot that slid through the net without even grazing the rim.

"Wow," Knight said, "who's that guy? He's good!"

Cody watched Terry Alston stand and admire his shot for a moment, then turn and lope downcourt with smooth, easy strides.

"That's Alston," he said. "Best athlete in the whole school. Just ask him. He transferred here from a private school in the Springs—Colorado Springs. He says basketball's his best sport. And, from what I've seen in gym class so far, he's probably right. We should be pretty good this year. We'll have a new coach. It should be fun."

Cody stopped talking. Knight had been nodding politely, like a bobble-head doll, but it was obvious he wasn't that interested in what kind of year the Grant basketball team would have.

Gotta shut up, Cody scolded himself, *before you bore this poor guy into a coma.*

He focused on the game again. Alston intercepted a lazy crosscourt pass and then dashed downcourt, sandy hair flying behind him. It looked like another easy layup for the shirts team.

Cody was startled when a huge blur streaked by. He thought he heard a cheerful "Check this!" as Pork Chop passed in front of him.

Alston slowed slightly as he zeroed in on the basket, sizing up a right-handed layup. As he released the ball, Pork Chop accelerated behind him. With a loud grunt, Chop propelled his 190 pounds into the air and extended his left arm.

He got just enough of his fingertips on the ball to direct it off the bottom of the backboard.

"Yeah! That's what I'm talkin' about!" Pork Chop's chest-deep bellow echoed off the gym walls. "How do you like that, TA? How do you like the taste of leather in the mornin'?"

Alston shot a glare at his much larger opponent. He retrieved the ball and then fired a hard chest pass at Pork Chop's stomach, but Chop caught the ball deftly and set it gently, almost lovingly, on the baseline.

"It's your ball, Hollywood," Chop said. "I swatted your mess outta there, remember?"

Cody could feel the tension building like the heat in a sauna. Pork Chop and Alston had been trash-talking since summer baseball. Now they stood only a few feet apart, staring each other down. Pork Chop's thick arms were folded across his chest, while Alston's hung at his sides, his hands clenching and unclenching.

When Coach Smith stepped between them, Cody felt a long exhale escape from his chest.

"You best save your aggression for the gridiron, Porter," Coach said evenly. "Besides, your team's down by four buckets. Not really a good time to be yappin'."

Alston went into his trademark sneer. "Yeah, Port—"

"And you," Coach Smith cut in, "don't even start with me, Blondie. You know, if you would have gone out for football, you two could have settled your differences on the field. But no, I guess some of us are just too pretty to play football, aren't we?"

Alston started to retort and then caught himself. Coach Smith shook his head and snorted. "I've had a gut full of this class. Run six laps and hit the showers."

On his way to the locker room, Pork Chop detoured toward Cody. "Did you check that block, Code?" he gushed. "Is the Midnight Cowboy the baddest baller in town or what? Do I not have crazy game? Am I not the king up in this beast?"

Cody rolled his eyes. "Yeah, Chop. You're bad. You're nationwide. If you can stop big-upping yourself for a minute, I want to introduce you to someone. This is Kris Knight, a new guy."

Pork Chop extended a meaty paw to Knight. "Welcome to Grant Penitentiary—I mean, Grant Middle School, new dude. Hey, did *you* see that block?"

"Uh-huh," Knight said nervously. "It was . . . uh . . . sweet!"

Pork Chop looked thoughtfully at the ceiling. Then he nodded slowly. "Interesting thought, there, Mr. Knight."

Cody sandwiched his head between his hands and started rubbing his temples. *Doesn't he ever get tired of this act?* he wondered.

"Sweet, swwwweeeet, suh-weet," Pork Chop said, playing with the word like a new toy. "Yeah, it was sweet, wasn't it? You're all right, new guy. You're gonna go far here. You're what I call . . . perceptive."

Knight smiled sheepishly. Cody stifled a groan.

Later that day, Cody and his rookie student sat across from each other at an eight-foot rectangular table near the lunchroom's exit doors. "Today's a good day, Kris," he said, dabbing mustard from the corners of his mouth. "The hot dogs here are pretty good. Of course, who could mess up a hot dog?"

Knight took a bite of his dog and nodded approvingly.

"But, dude, I gotta warn you. You must beware of the grilled-cheese sandwiches in this place. It's this DayGlo orange stuff that must come from radioactive cows or something."

Cody felt the table shiver as Pork Chop plopped down across the table from him. "Yeah," he said, "Code's right about the sammiches. They upset my tummy big-time. Gives whole new meaning to that slogan about 'the power of cheese!' The power to make you hurl!"

"True," Cody said, gulping from a carton of chocolate milk. "But if you really wanna talk gut-bomb food, you gotta talk lasagna. Under no circumstances should you eat the lasagna here. You'll get heartburn."

Pork Chop belched in agreement. "Dude, if I were stranded on a desert island and had a choice between eating the school's lasagna or my own foot, well, they'd have to start calling me Hopalong!"

Knight covered his mouth with his napkin, fighting to keep his milk where it belonged. Cody saw his eyes begin to water.

Pork Chop clapped Knight on the back so hard that he began to cough. "A man with a sense of humor? I like you already, dude. It's hard to find people in this little town who can appreciate my sophisticated wit."

"Well, he's not going to be able to appreciate your humor if you kill the poor guy with those sledge-hammer arms of yours," Cody said. "Take it easy, okay? The man's trying to eat."

It looked to Cody like Pork Chop was forming an apology when the sharp call of "Mr. Porter!" cut through the chatter and clatter of 127 dining eighth graders. It was Mrs. Studdard, the lunchroom monitor—or Lunch Nazi, as Pork Chop affectionately called her.

"You know the rules here, Mr. Porter. Off with the cowboy hat! Now!"

Pork Chop nodded politely at Mrs. Studdard. He removed his black Stetson, blew some imaginary dust off of it, and, as if it were made of eggshells, set it beside his lunch tray.

Mrs. Studdard sighed heavily. "And the do-rag, too, Mr. Porter."

Pork Chop groaned loudly. "Aw, Missus S, can't a brother get some love?"

"Not in my lunchroom, Mr. Porter. I've no time for love. You want love? Go find a girlfriend!"

That brought hoots and squeals from many of Pork Chop's fellow diners.

"But, Missus S.," he said, rising as if he were a defense lawyer in the trial of the century, "you can't take my cuh-BOY hat and my do-rag. I'm the Midnight Cowboy!"

Mrs. Studdard tilted her head toward the ceiling, as if seeking divine strength from above. "You'll have to be the Midnight Cowboy on your own time—and somewhere other than my lunchroom. You want to wear something on your head, I'll get you a hairnet and you can start helping us serve lunch. I bet you'd look real cute in a hairnet, Mr. Porter."

More hooting and a few whistles followed this proclamation. Pork Chop looked around the room, smiling. He removed his do-rag, placed it on top of his cowboy hat, bowed to Mrs. Studdard, and sat down.

Chapter 2
Living with Pain

Blake Randall turned off his boom box and wheeled his chair from behind his desk to a spot five feet in front of the metal folding chair where Cody sat.

Cody looked around the cramped rectangular office, which was about half the size of Pastor Taylor's. He wondered if the youth pastor's salary was half that of the senior pastor's as well. One of the longer walls was lined with bookshelves, most packed with Blake's collection of tattered paperbacks, featuring authors like Lewis, McDowell, Schaeffer, Colson, Buechner, Tozer, and Calvin. Cody recognized a few of the authors from his parents' own literary collection. His mom had done most of the book reading, sometimes enticing his dad to do a Bible study with her. But he hadn't seen Luke Martin read anything but the newspaper, the *Wall Street Journal,* and *Business Week* since Mom died.

For the past two months, Dad's black leather Bible sat on his nightstand, usually underneath a coffee cup or reading glasses. Mom never would have stood for that. She had told him hundreds of times, "The Bible is God's holy Word. It isn't a coaster or a footrest. And it's the best book there is, so nothing should ever go on top of it. Not even a book by Billy Graham or Francis Schaeffer or Max Lucado."

Cody noticed that Blake's bookshelves held at least a half-dozen Bibles. They were on the top shelf. *Mom would approve,* he thought. The bottom shelf featured Blake's hardcover, thick-as-a-brick Bible commentaries—on every book in the Old and New Testaments. "My doorstops," he jokingly called them.

The other long wall was home to Blake's CD collection, the envy of every kid at the church. He had ordered the hundreds of CDs alphabetically, from Audio Adrenaline to ZOEgirl.

Blake called his books and music his "soul food." He once told Cody, "If I ever have to go live on a desert island, this is all I'm takin' with me—my tunes and my tomes."

After Blake had explained to Cody that "tome" meant a book, Cody laughed with the same sportsmanship he tried to show a losing team after a game.

Cody turned his attention from the walls to his young youth director, only two years out of college, now intently flipping through the yellow pages of a thick legal pad.

"So," Blake said deliberately, "how was your week?"

Cody let his gaze fall to the well-worn carpet. It was a faded sky blue, with pinkish flecks, as if someone had splattered Pepto-Bismol across it.

"It was okay, I guess, B. We lost to Central in our season opener. And I got rocked big-time. This dude named Tucker blindsided me. Coach says I need to get tougher."

Blake sat back in his chair. It looked to Cody like he had finally found the page he was looking for.

"Well, Code, you have Holy Family this afternoon. That should get you one in the win column."

"We're in trouble if it doesn't. Coach will have us doing wind sprints for a week."

"Your dad going to make it to the game today?"

Cody let a long, slow breath escape his lungs. "You'd have to ask him. But I wouldn't put money on it. You know, Mom never missed a home game. And she came to almost every away game, too. When it got cold toward the end of football season, she wore this big old red down coat. It made it easy to pick her out in the stands. She looked like a giant tomato."

Cody waited for Blake to finish chuckling before continuing.

"It wasn't the same last week, without her in the bleachers. I was trying to focus, trying to play a smart game. But I felt hollow inside. It was hard to breathe sometimes. It reminded me of when Chop and I were kids and he used to sit on my chest. I don't know— maybe that's why I got knocked on my can. Too much on my mind."

Blake forced a smile. It looked more like a grimace to Cody. "Maybe today will be better. I'll be in the stands, pulling for you." He held his pen like a chopstick and began drumming on his pad. "Let's leave football for a while, okay? I'd like to know how you're doing, emotionally, and especially spiritually."

Cody let his head tilt back until he heard his neck crackle. "I don't know, B. Not very well. It just hurts that she's not here anymore. I almost started crying in science class yesterday, right in the middle of a lesson on photosynthesis. It just kinda hits me hard sometimes. It takes me by surprise.

"It's crazy, too. On Monday I got an A on my math quiz, and I started thinking, I can't wait to get home and show this to Mom. I was thinking how excited she'd be because, as you know, getting an A isn't exactly an everyday thing for me—especially not in math. I swear, it was a good five minutes before it hit me: You can't tell her, you idiot, she's dead."

Blake's eyes were moist. "I'm sorry, Cody," he said quietly.

"Yeah, me too. You know, the same thing happened in baseball this summer. It was the last game of the season, and I got my first over-the-fence homer ever. I was thinking that I would call her collect, because the game was up in Denver. She always said, 'You do something special in any game when I'm not there in person, you call me ASAP, collect!'"

Cody shook his head slowly from side to side. "I'm at a phone booth outside 7-Eleven, I had the number half dialed before reality hit me. Am I crazy, Blake? Am I in, what do they call it—"

"Denial?"

"Yeah, denial."

"I don't think so, Code. I've been reading a lot about grief. What you're experiencing is not all that uncommon. Having someone you love around you every day and then having that person taken away suddenly—it's a shock to the system. Have you talked to your dad about how you feel?"

"I tried once. He just said—from behind his *Wall Street Journal* I might add—'Old habits die hard.'

What's that supposed to mean, anyway? And I've asked him to pray with me a couple of times, but he just points his finger at the ceiling and snaps, 'I have nothing to say to him!' But other times, I'll see dad kneeling by his bed or with his hands folded at the dinner table—like's he's gotta be praying. What's up with that, B? It's like I'm living with two different people!"

"I think your dad is really struggling. Imagine having cancer steal the most important person in your life."

"I don't have to imagine. That's what I face every day. It happened to me, too, Blake!"

Cody felt the hot tears rolling down his face. "I hate this," he said.

"It's okay to show your emotions, Cody."

"I've shown them way too often. I couldn't even speak for Mom at the funeral because I was terrified of making a blubbering fool of myself. And now I'm afraid I'll start crying at football practice someday. That would be the worst. Coach Smith would have a field day with me. I don't even want to think about what he'd say."

"Does it matter what he'd say?"

Cody threw the question around in his mind, as if he were tossing pop flies to himself. He looked Blake in the eye.

"It's not so much what Coach or anybody else says. It's just that what's happening to me—I don't understand it. I mean, is it going to be like this for the rest of my whole stupid life?"

"I don't think so. I don't think you'll keep running for the phone every time you hit a homer or sink a game-winning free throw. And I don't think the tears will sneak up on you so frequently."

"Well, that's good, I guess. But I don't want to forget about her either."

Blake studied his legal pad for a moment. "You won't, Cody. Remember what Pastor Taylor said at the funeral: Death ends a life on earth; it doesn't end a relationship. Linda Martin will always be your mom. And I'm not just talking about memories and all that. All the love she invested in you is part of who you are. It always will be."

"Yeah. I'll try harder to remember that. I just wish I could still share stuff with her. Like if we won today, we'd go to Mamie's House of Pies or Dairy Delight to celebrate. Chop and I would tell her all about our favorite plays. We'd answer all of her questions. I'm going to miss that."

"Maybe you don't need to miss it."

"What!? You just lost me, B."

"You can still tell your mom how you did. My grandpa, my dad's dad, he died ten years ago, and my pops still goes to his grave a couple times a year. They have 'conversations,' although I'm sure they're pretty one-sided. You can do that too."

"But isn't that kinda weird? I mean, it's like praying to a dead person or something."

Blake held up his right palm, like a traffic cop. "I never said anything about praying to her—just sharing what's on your heart."

"And that's okay? It's not a sin or anything?"

"Not that I know of."

Cody glanced at his watch and rose slowly. Game time was only three hours away. "I'll think about what you've said, B. But I'm not sure if I can still talk to Mom or not."

Blake stood and extended his hand. "It's okay if you don't. I can't say if it's right for you."

"Right now, I'm not even sure, B, and I'm ... well ... me. Besides, it opens up a whole can of questions."

"Anything I can help with?"

"I don't think so. Not right now, anyway." Cody tapped his head with his forefinger. "Right now there are so many questions bouncing around in here—and with a lot of them, I'm not sure I even *want* to know the answers."

"Well, you know where to find me. I don't have all the answers. I'm still learning, just as you are. But I'll always try."

Blake released Cody from their handshake and pushed him gently on the shoulder. "Now get home and get ready to tear 'em up on the field today."

At lunch the Monday following the Holy Family game, Pork Chop plopped next to Cody with his customary impact. Cody glanced up from his macaroni and cheese—or "macaroni and cheese-like substance," as Pork Chop called it.

"Nice of you to join us, Chop."

Chop began prying open his carton of chocolate milk with his thick fingers. "Yeah, I know." He looked across the table at Kris Knight. "Hey, new guy, how you livin'?"

Knight nodded. "Okay."

"You come to the game last week?"

Knight looked like a mouse cornered by a cat. "Uh—no."

Pork Chop frowned. "What, you don't like football or something? Are you from this country?"

Cody sighed loudly. "It's okay, Kris," he interjected. "Chop, back off, okay? Not everybody has to like football. It's still a free country, you know."

Pork Chop chugged his half pint of chocolate milk, then crushed the carton in his right fist. He belched thoughtfully and looked at Knight. "It's cool if you're not into football, new guy. But you missed it by not being there on Saturday." He clapped Cody on the back. "Because my boy here made the play of the season!"

Cody dipped his head and tried not to smile.

"Really?" Knight asked. "What did you do, Cody?"

"I'll tell you," Pork Chop said. "You know what a wedge is, right?"

Knight cocked his head. "A wedgie?"

Pork Chop shook his head in disbelief. "No, not a wedgie. Where did you say you were from, anyway? Never mind. Allow me to demonstrate."

He slid his lunch tray aside, grabbed the salt and pepper shakers from the center of the table, and set them in front of him. He studied the gray and white plastic containers, his forehead wrinkled in a frown. "Hey, Bart," Pork Chop called to the far end of the table, "slide me your pepper, dude."

Bart Evans stopped his conversation with his twin brother, Brett, who was seated across from him. "Porter, you already have pepper. Right in front of you."

"Bart," Chop said in a forced-calm voice that always made Cody nervous, "please pass me your pepper. Come on, you're our QB. You should like to pass stuff. Besides, I need it for educational purposes. Don't make me come down there and get it. I thought you were the smart twin."

"Whatever, Porter," Bart said wearily, as he slid the container down the table.

"Okay," Chop said, the excitement building in his voice as he arranged the shakers side by side. "This, new guy, is a wedge. See, when you kick off, three or four guys from the opposing team form a wedge so they can block for the kick return. In this particular case, it was a three-man wedge." He paused and placed the crumpled milk carton behind the three shakers. "Holy Family, their return guy, Mack, is white—and this is a chocolate-milk carton—so this isn't what you would call a totally accurate re-creation, but you get the point, right?"

Knight nodded obediently.

Chop snatched a half-eaten sugar cookie from Cody's tray. "Done with this?"

Cody stared at his friend, mouth open. "Uh, I guess I am now."

"Cool. So, now my expert game analysis will continue. This cookie is Cody, right? We kick off to open the game." He stopped to look at his tray, then Cody's. "Crud, it's too bad we aren't having lima beans today. One of those bad boys woulda made a perfect football. But that's okay. We'll just use our imaginations. Anyway, so here comes the imaginary football to Mack, who's got crazy wheels. He gets behind the wedge, just like he's supposed to, and they charge upfield."

Chop paused and looked down the table at the Evans twins. "Brett Evans," he said, clearing his throat loudly, "our alleged wedge buster, gets knocked on his skinny booty, and it looks like this could be a big return. Mack is picking up speed."

He stopped again to advance the condiment shakers and milk carton across the table, toward Knight. "But then," Pork Chop said, lowering his voice for dramatic effect, "here comes my boy, Cody Martin, charging straight at the wedge. I'm watching from the sideline, and it looks like a suicide mission to me. I mean, one on three? They're gonna squash him, right?"

Knight shrugged. "Um, I guess so?"

Pork Chop smiled. "I thought so, too. But, dude, check this." He moved the half cookie into position in front of the shakers. "My boy, he dives, head first, like he's Rickey Henderson stealing second base! He mows down all three wedge guys like they're bowling pins!" Chop rammed his cookie-filled hand into the shakers and watched in wonder as they rattled and spun across the table. The salt decanter eventually rolled to Knight's side of the table and tumbled to the floor.

Chop now had the attention of the nearby tables, so he raised his voice another level. "And that's not all! Somehow, in the middle of the flyin' bodies, Code gets a hand on Mack's right foot and sends him sprawling. One second, Mack thinks he's takin' the return all the way to the house, the next he's eatin' turf!" He picked up the milk carton and spiked it on the table for emphasis. Then he slammed both palms on the table. Silverware clattered. Water sloshed out of Cody's drink cup. Are y'all feelin' this? He takes out four guys! It was fierce! HF's coach is screaming on the far sideline—he thinks it should be a penalty or something. I look behind me, and the home crowd is going nuts!"

Pork Chop looked up and saw Mrs. Studdard coming toward him, so he began talking rapid-fire, "And Coach Smith, who doesn't usually get excited unless he's mad, he's whoopin' and pumping his fist like Tiger Woods. He's so amped I think he's gonna blow a breaker! He turns to Coach Benton, the assistant coach, and says, 'I guess we're gonna have to start calling Martin 'Cody Crash'!"

Cody had bowed his head for the entire demonstration. He raised it now and saw Knight staring at him, his eyes radiating admiration. "That's awesome, Cody. Wish I could have been there to see it."

Cody shrugged. "Well, it was only one play."

"You're way too modest, man," Chop said. "You heard what Coach Smith said in the locker room after we won, twelve-zip, 'That play set the tone for the whole game.'" Pork Chop paused for a moment and studied the remains of Cody's cookie. "Homeboy," he said, "you want your cookie back?"

"Uh, no."

Pork Chop raised his eyebrows plaintively. "Well? You sure?"

Cody shook his head. "Help yourself."

Pork Chop picked up the cookie remnant and tossed it in his mouth. "It's a shame to waste good food, you know. There are people starving in Indiana."

"India," Cody said wearily.

"There too!"

"Give it back!" a sharp female voice Cody knew too well interrupted the conversation. He twisted around and saw Robyn, two tables down. Andrew Neale had stolen the cookie from her plate and stood over her, dangling it above her head. "I'm not kidding, Neale!" her voice was measured, but intense. "Give it back!"

"How bad do you want it?" Neale taunted in his low nasal voice.

Pork Chop smiled grimly as he pushed himself up from the table. "You gonna rescue your woman, Code, or you want me to do it?"

"She's *not* my woman," Cody snapped, surprised at the anger in his voice.

Pork Chop's smile widened. "Yeah, right."

Cody rose to his feet and drew in a deep breath. He felt his heart accelerating.

Please, God, he prayed silently, *please show me what to do. And, if it would be your will, please don't let me get beaten to a pulp in front of the whole lunchroom. Especially not in front of Robyn when I'm tryin' to rescue her. Amen.*

He followed Pork Chop to Robyn's table. Neale was still taunting her, passing the cookie back and forth between his left and right hands.

Cody saw Neale's sarcastic smile turn to a wince when a set of bony fingers clamped around the back of his neck.

"Andrew Neale," Mrs. Studdard said evenly, "how nice of you to volunteer for cleanup duty."

Neale started to protest, but Mrs. Studdard countered by cupping her other hand over his mouth. "I must advise you, Mr. Neale, anything you say can and will be used against you in a court of law. And this," she said, slowly rotating her head to take in the expanse of the lunchroom, "is my courtroom. And I ... I am the law. Do you understand me?"

Cody saw Neale's head bobbing up and down, but he wasn't sure if the nod was voluntary or controlled by Mrs. Studdard. "That's a good boy." She chuckled. "Now get back to the kitchen and ask Doris for an apron. I think she has one your size—extra gangly."

As Neale trudged away, Mrs. Studdard turned her attention to Robyn. "Go get yourself another cookie, sweetie," she said warmly. "We don't know where Mr. Neale's hands have been. In fact, take two."

Pork Chop looked at Cody and shrugged as they returned to their table. "Dude, Mrs. S has got game!" he said. "Who knew?"

Cody, Pork Chop, and Knight watched Robyn get her replacement cookies from Mrs. Ward, one of the servers. Then she turned, pushed her frameless Perry Ellis glasses with the pink-tinted lenses up on her short, narrow nose, and marched to her seat. She flashed Cody a quick, coy smile as she sat down.

"So," Knight began warily, "is that your girlfriend, Cody?"

Pork Chop began rubbing his palms together furiously, as if trying to create enough friction to start a fire. "Oh, I gotta hear this answer!" he said.

Cody drummed his fingertips nervously on the tabletop. "Robyn Hart is *not* my girlfriend, okay? We're friends. That's all. Friends."

Pork Chop fake-coughed. "Friends, huh? I didn't know friends kissed!"

"That was in the fifth grade, Chop. And it was on a dare! For cryin' out loud, when are you gonna stop throwing that in my face?"

Pork Chop stroked his chin thoughtfully. "Not any time soon. It's too much fun."

"Hey," said Knight, mercifully changing the subject, "who was that skinny dude who was harassing, uh, Robyn?"

Cody heard himself groan. "Andrew Neale. Biggest pain in the school. He harasses everybody."

Pork Chop cleared his throat loudly.

Cody smiled. "Well, almost everybody. He gets by with it because he's best friends with Alston. He's roughest on the girls. Especially this one named Greta."

"Who stinks like three-day-old road kill," Pork Chop interjected.

"Chop, please, give her a break!"

"I'd rather give her a bar of soap—and some of that stuff that's strong enough for a man, but made for a woman!"

Cody rolled his eyes. "Whatever. Anyway, Kris, watch your back around Neale."

"But," Pork Chop added, "if he hassles you, just let me know. I'll take care of it."

Cody raised his eyebrows. "You gonna take care of Alston too?"

Pork Chop waved his hand in front of his face as if shooing mosquitoes. "One of these days, my brother. One of these days, Terry Alston is going to meet my two friends."

"Two friends?" Knight asked.

"Oh, yeah," Pork Chop said, with mock solemnity, holding up his left fist, "my friend Six Months in the Hospital—" he paused for dramatic effect before holding up his right fist "—and my other friend Sudden Death!"

Mrs. Studdard waited for Pork Chop to lower Sudden Death before she grabbed him by the wrist, tugging its owner to his feet. "If you're quite through, Mr. Porter," she said cheerfully, "your assistance is required to help clean tabletops and sweep the floors."

Pork Chop gave her a wounded look. "Why? What did I do?"

"I saw that little football dramatization you put on. Haven't you been taught not to play with your food?"

"Well, technically, it was Code's food—oww! I'm trying to explain something here! Don't you wanna hear my defense?"

Smiling, Mrs. Studdard had moved her grip from Pork Chop's right wrist to his right ear. She began leading him slowly to the rear of the lunchroom. "Well," she said, "I'd love to hear your defense, but you better tell your story walkin'!"

Pork Chop called to Cody as he was led away, "Dude, if I'm not out of here by the time practice starts, send a rescue party!"

Cody tried to suppress a laugh. Mrs. Studdard was handing Pork Chop a sponge and a pail of water. "This can't be good for my hands, Mrs. S," he said loudly enough for the entire lunchroom to hear. "If my shooting touch is messed up come basketball season, I'm gonna sue!"

Mrs. Studdard scoffed, "What touch, Mr. Porter? I've seen blacksmiths with a softer touch than yours."

Pork Chop held his hand—sponge included—over his heart. "Oooooh! That's harsh!" He called to Cody once more. "If I don't make it outta here alive, you gotta keep my memory goin', man. Don't let 'em forget the Midnight Cowboy!"

Cody gave Chop a quick salute, then turned to Knight. "Let's get out of here, dude, before we get forced to help him."

Knight scrunched up his nose. "Well, shouldn't you help him? I mean, you are his friend."

Cody let his jaw drop. "Are you kidding?" he asked. "He ruined my cookie! Now c'mon, we're so outta here!"

The week of practices went quickly. The team scrimmaged on Wednesday, and Cody earned two congratulatory slaps on his helmet from Coach Smith. The first was for sacking Mark Goddard, the second-string quarterback, on a broken play.

Goddard couldn't find a receiver on a pass play, so he had scrambled out of the pocket, to his right. He had just planted his right foot to turn upfield when Cody arrived on the scene. He squared his shoulders, arched his back, and charged forward, remembering to keep his head up.

Goddard lost momentum when he tried to cut, and he toppled like a bowling pin when Cody hit him head-on. He wrapped his arms around Goddard's torso and drove him onto his back. Goddard hit the ground with a loud "Ooo!" as the wind was driven from him.

Coach Smith whistled the play dead and trotted over to Cody. "Did you all see that hit?" he asked excitedly. "Did you see how Cody Crash wrapped up his man and tried to plant him in the turf? That's the kind of hittin' I want to see out here!"

Cody slid off Goddard and stood, offering him his hand.

"Good . . . hit," Goddard gasped, as he pulled himself to his feet.

Coach Smith was still rattling on about the sack as the two units huddled up. "That's the way you do it," he said. "You don't nudge a guy with your shoulder. This ain't bumper cars. You drive through your man,

you wrap him up, and you put him on his back! You
know what? That was a good way to end the scrimmage. You can break outta your huddles. And because
I'm in such a good mood, no wind sprints tonight!"

That announcement brought whoops from most of
the team. Several players came up to clap Cody across
the shoulder pads as he and Pork Chop jogged to the
locker room.

The Friday before the Mill Creek game was
Cody's last day as Kris Knight's official mentor and
tour guide. At lunchtime, they took their customary seats and picked warily at their grilled-cheese
sandwiches.

"So," Cody said, "how is school going for you
so far?"

"It's all right. Grant is bigger than my old school in
Kansas."

"I guess I never asked—what made you move to
Colorado?"

"My dad's job. He's an engineer in the Springs. My
mom stays home to watch over my little sister and
stuff. She's two. What do your parents do?"

Cody fidgeted. Everyone always said parents, plural.
"My dad works in the Springs, just like yours," he
said. "He's a business writer for the newspaper."

"And your mom?"

Cody felt the familiar lump forming in his throat, the familiar knot tightening in his stomach. "Um, she died this past summer. Cancer."

Knight looked embarrassed to the point of nausea. He trained his eyes on his tray as he mumbled: "Oh. Uh—I'm sorry. I had no idea—"

"It's okay," Cody said, because he didn't know what else to say. He scanned the lunchroom as awkward seconds crawled by. Where was Chop when you needed him?

Cody was replaying the uncomfortable lunchroom exchange as Grant lined up to receive the opening kickoff from Mill Creek on an oven-like Saturday afternoon. He recalled the pained expression on Knight's face. He'd seen that look at least a hundred times when an innocent question led to an unexpected answer. Each time it happened, he feared the feeble dam that was holding back a lake of tears would give way.

Sometimes it did. He'd already made three trips to the nurse's office, and it was only a month into the school year. As he scanned the field for someone to block, he wondered how long the excuses of stomach aches and headaches would work. He wondered if someday he wouldn't make it out of a classroom before the tears escaped, before his cover was blown.

Cody was imagining what Andrew Neale would say in such an instance when a Mill Creek defender drove a shoulder into his stomach. The impact was so severe that he felt his teeth sinking deep into his rubber mouth guard. For a moment, he feared he might bite through it. Then he noticed that he was airborne. At first it was a peaceful feeling. He noted small tufts of clouds in the sky as he fell backward.

Then the clouds were gone. It was as if he were watching TV and someone yanked the plug out of the wall. He felt his head bounce on the turf. Everything clicked to black.

Cody opened his eyes. The array of helmets, arms, and legs above him seemed out of proportion, as if he were looking in a fun-house mirror or having one of his pepperoni pizza-induced wild dreams. Instinctively, he tried to scramble to his feet, but his body didn't seem to be under his complete control.

He felt like a novice puppeteer trying to maneuver a complex, unfamiliar marionette. A guy from Creek appeared above him. He pulled his U-shaped guard from his mouth. "How'd you like that hit, forty-one?" he spat. "You gonna go cry to your mama now?"

Cody blinked his eyes and tried to decipher the meaning of his opponent's taunts. He felt like he should be angry, but no anger burned inside him. "What?" he said in a bewildered voice. "What did you say?"

"I called you a mama's boy! What—you got sod in your ears?"

Cody blinked some more. "Mama's boy," he said softly to himself. Then he felt his anger heating up.

It's time to get up and clock this guy, he thought.

Cody lifted his head from the field. It felt as if it weighed a hundred pounds. Frustrated, he lowered it back down.

As soon as I can move again, you're a dead man, number 53, he vowed. *If I can move again.*

Now one of the three referees was bent over him. "You okay, son?" he asked.

The next thing he knew, Cody was on his feet. Pork Chop's hand was on his back, steering him toward the sideline. He wondered if he had answered the ref's question.

Coach Smith was waiting for him, arms crossed, eyes blazing. "Martin!" he snarled. "For heaven's sake, get your pickin' head in the game! What's wrong with you? I thought you were a man. But if you're gonna play football like a little kid, I suggest you turn in your gear and go find a swing set!"

Cody stared at his coach for a moment. He was shocked by the possible responses that were echoing in his head. Any one of them would get him kicked off the team for sure.

Dear God, he prayed fervently, *please help me keep these words that are inside my head right now* inside *my head!*

When Coach turned his attention from Cody to argue an offside call with one of the refs, Cody grabbed the opportunity and slipped away to the end of the line of Raiders who stood watching the game, standing side by side between the twenty-five yard lines.

As the static in his head dissipated, Cody looked across the field, trying to find number 53. As he blinked back tears, uninvited words flashed in his mind in large, capital, movie marquee letters: MAMA'S BOY. LITTLE KID. SWING SET. WEAK. BABY. SOFT. PUNK. He tried to force them out of his head, but they only loomed brighter and bigger, taunting him.

He unsnapped his chin guard and removed his helmet, hoping that would clear his mind. Suddenly, his eyes locked on number 53, who was pointing at him from across the field and laughing as he said something to a teammate.

Cody quickly put his helmet back on. *Just wait till I get back in the game, fifty-three,* he seethed. *I'm puttin' a big hurt on you.*

He felt tears slithering down his face. But that was okay. It was a blistering day. He hoped everyone would think they were drops of sweat.

Cody stood on the sidelines and watched Mill Creek methodically march downfield for a touchdown. The Marauders wisely avoided the middle of the Grant line—and Pork Chop—and stuck to running sweeps and short out-patterns.

On Grant's next offensive possession, Bart Evans underthrew his twin brother on an out-pattern and suffered his first interception of the young season. Mill Creek took over on the Raiders' forty-one yard line.

On first down, the Marauders ran a QB sweep to the left. Back in the game now, Cody felt his heart race as he chased the play. A Creek blocker took Brett Evans out along the left sideline, leaving Cody one-on-one with Mike Riley, the QB, who lowered his head and charged forward. Cody kept his head up and tried to square his shoulders, preparing for a mighty collision.

Then something flashed through his mind. It wasn't an image, but the split-second memory of the hit he had taken against Central. Reflexively, Cody looked to his right, fearing another blocker ear-holing him from the blind side.

But the hit came head-on. He felt Riley's face mask plunge into his gut and then he felt himself tumbling backward. He hoped the impact would at least trip up Riley, but he knew that wasn't the case, even before he rolled from his back to his stomach and watched the QB scamper into the end zone.

This time, Coach Smith didn't even speak to Cody as he reached the sideline. He merely folded his arms and turned his back.

Grant was able to answer with a long drive of its own. Halfback Marcus Berringer cut the Mill Creek lead to a touchdown with a one-yard plunge.

After Creek returned the kickoff to its own thirty-three, Cody buckled his chinstrap and headed onto the field to join the defense. But Coach Smith grabbed him from behind, by the shoulder pads, and spun him around.

"No, Martin! You stay here with me, where it's safe. A baby like you could get hurt out there."

Cody glared at his coach, who sneered at him and then turned away. "Betts," he barked, "get in there and play monster for Martin."

On the bus ride home, Cody sat alone in the rear seat. He barely moved for the forty-five-minute trip, his eyes boring into the seat ahead of him. No one attempted to talk to him, not even Pork Chop.

Grant had won the game, 21-17, but Cody felt no joy, no sense of accomplishment. He felt only anger at Coach Smith.

The next week, Grant bumped its record to 3-1 with a win at Maranatha Christian School. Cody played only on special teams and missed an open-field tackle on a punt return. He expected Coach Smith to scream at him when he went to the sideline, but the coach just shook his head disgustedly.

Betts, who missed half of his attempted tackles because he closed his eyes on impact, seemed well on his way to becoming the team's new monster back, despite his shortcomings.

In the following Wednesday's scrimmage, Cody got no repetitions on defense, not even with the second team. As he trudged home from practice, he decided to tell his father about what was happening.

Maybe Dad will talk to Coach Smith, he thought. *Maybe it takes an adult to talk sense into another adult. Betts is killing us at monster, and Coach doesn't even seem to care. Besides, is Coach forgetting what happened to me this summer? Doesn't he have any sympathy at all?*

He was surprised to see his dad's car in the driveway at 5:30. Luke Martin had been putting in heavy overtime lately. It wasn't like when his wife was alive and family dinner was at six o'clock sharp every night—unless Cody had a game or a meet. In those cases, they would stop for a burger afterwards. Often, a few of Cody's fellow athletes and their parents would join them.

Cody entered the front door. The television was tuned to CNN. Dad sat in his large black recliner, head buried in his slender hands. Cody couldn't hear much over the din of a correspondent giving a report from "war-torn" someplace or other, but from the way his father's head and torso trembled, he was probably crying.

Cody slipped quietly upstairs to his room. He hadn't seen his dad cry since the day of the funeral.

Chapter 3
Hungry for Action

On the first Friday afternoon in October, Grant traveled to Lincoln. The team was smarting after a one-point loss to Cook—in which Cody played only on the kickoff and extra-point teams.

By the end of the first half of the Lincoln game, Cody had seen action on a grand total of three plays. One kickoff and two punts. The second half wasn't much better. Coach Smith let him play monster on the Raiders' final defensive effort, but Lincoln, up 23-3, ran two lackluster off-tackle plays, then had Locke, their QB, kneel in the backfield to run out the clock. Cody didn't even bother to shower after the game.

I worked up a better sweat during the history test last week, he thought as he changed out of his uniform.

Before he left the locker room to head for the bus, Cody found Pork Chop, who was muttering something about "complete and total disgrace" as he unwound tattered white athletic tape from his left wrist.

"Chop?" he asked tentatively, "I need to talk to you on the bus, okay? It's important."

Pork Chop looked up, studying his friend's face. "Okay, Code." He sighed. "All the cheerleaders are fighting over who should sit by me, but I guess I might as well break all their hearts."

"This is about playing time, isn't it," Pork Chop said, as he shucked the wrapper off a Snickers bar.

Cody wearily punched the seat in front of him. "More like a *lack* of playing time. Chop, I'm thinking of quitting the team."

Cody thought Pork Chop was going to spit peanuts, caramel, and chocolate all over himself.

"Are you trippin'?" Chop said. "This is four years we've been playing together. We've been the heart of every defense we've been on—even back in Bantams. Dude, you love football!"

"I know, Chop. But I love *playing* football, not watching it from the sidelines. If I just want to be a spectator, I've got the Broncos, or your brother and the high school team. It just hurts too much to stand around."

Pork Chop crumpled his candy bar wrapper and stuffed it into the pocket of his blue jeans. "You'll get some PT soon. You're just in Coach Smith's doghouse right now. It's happened to everybody. He even benched Berringer in the second half today for not hitting the holes fast enough."

"Yeah, but Coach usually lightens up once he's made his point. But with me, it's like he's going for a world-record grudge or something. Has he forgotten about all the good stuff I did earlier in the season? Is he senile or what? I think he hates me now. I don't know if I'll ever get any real playing time. It's like I'm trapped in his doghouse. And I don't need this kinda stuff in my life right now, know what I'm sayin'?" He buried his head in his hands and admitted quietly, "I miss her. I miss her every single day."

Pork Chop sat back in his seat, studying the back of Coach Smith's head seven rows in front of them. "I feel what you're sayin'. Want me to say something to Coach?"

Cody shook his head furiously. "No way, Chop. That just seems all wrong to me. Besides, it would probably just make things worse."

"It's your choice, man. But just don't quit, okay? I know that you don't roll like that. Besides, if you quit football, how are we going to play for the Broncos someday? Now *that* would make your mom proud."

Cody sighed. "Well, maybe it'll be just you playing for them. Me, I'll probably be the water boy or something. That's about what I am now. When I think about what I hoped this season would be—and how it really is—I just want to put my fist through a wall!"

A sly smile crept across Pork Chop's face. "You're mad, huh? Sometimes I play my best when I'm mad."

Cody walked home from school. Pork Chop's brother, Doug, had offered him a ride, but he declined, saying, "I might as well get some exercise today."

He saw his Dad through the front window, rooted to his recliner and parked in front of the TV as usual. Cody didn't feel like talking to him about the game— or anything—so he quietly raised the garage door and slipped inside. He sat on the weight-lifting bench that occupied one side of the two-car garage. The garage smelled of gasoline and stale grass clippings. He flopped onto his back, staring at the rough-hewn beams that crisscrossed the ceiling. He closed his eyes and remembered the last time he had spent any quality time in the garage.

It was late summer, two weeks after his mother's funeral. He had sat on the concrete floor, plucking chunks of mud, and brittle, yellowed, year-old grass from between the rubber cleats of his football shoes. They had felt loose during the seventh grade season, even with two pairs of thick socks, so he hoped they would fit his eighth grade feet perfectly. He had heard his dad complaining on the phone about the cost of the funeral. He didn't want to add new football cleats to the equation.

Cody sighed. He remembered holding one of the shoes up to his face. The smell reminded him of the hay on Pork Chop's farm. That, in turn, brought images of games of H-O-R-S-E in the Porter family driveway, sprint races down the long dirt road that led to their farm, and he and Chop spotting Doug as he bench-pressed extraordinary amounts of weight in the basement-turned-workout room.

Cody swung his legs off the bench and rose wearily to his feet. He wagged his head sadly. That day seemed so long ago. And so much had changed. Even with the burden of his mother's death weighing down his soul, he had felt hope that day as he thought of the upcoming football season.

He had reason to be hopeful then. He was hurting, but football was the sport that let you wear armor. There was a pad or support for almost every body part. And the helmet, that was the best of all. It let you crash into ball carriers or take head slaps from opposing blockers without getting your brains scrambled.

Putting on a football uniform was like a superhero changing into his costume and assuming a new identity. It transformed you—made you bigger and more powerful than you were in civilian clothes. Once in the crimson and white colors of Grant Middle School, he was no longer Cody Martin, skinny kid with a Santa Claus-size bag of insecurities and fears. He was Cody Martin, Monster Back.

Most importantly, during the hours of drills, scrimmages, and games—especially the games—he could often shake himself free from the pain of his mother's death.

He thought about what Chop had said on the bus, "I play best when I'm mad." That made sense. Maybe that's where he had gone wrong. He'd lost the fire. He thought about what Coach Smith had called him.

"Little kid," he whispered through gritted teeth. "I'll show you little kid." He picked up a ten-pound weight-lifting plate from the floor, cupped it in his right hand like a discus. Then, with a war cry that he was sure his dad would hear, even over the bluster of CNN, he hurled the weight into the garage drywall. The plate clunked to the floor, and Cody smiled as he saw the deep gouge it made in the wall. He felt the adrenaline coursing through his body.

"I wish it were game time right now," he said, "because I am through being hurt. It's time to make someone else hurt!"

He stood in the center of the garage, waiting for his dad to come charging in from the kitchen. *If he asks what happened*, Cody thought, *I'll tell him exactly what happened. I'll say, "I got mad and chucked a dime into the wall. So what?"*

But his dad never showed up.

After several minutes of stalking back and forth across the length of the garage, Cody went to the door that connected the garage to the kitchen and quietly slipped inside. He made his way to the living room, taking slow, deliberate steps.

Dad's *Wall Street Journal* lay across his lap. CNN was showing baseball highlights, but his dad would never know that the Yankees beat the Red Sox in extra innings. His head was tilted back to the ceiling, and he was snoring loudly. He sounded like one of the tractors on the Porter farm.

Man, Cody thought, *he must be tired if he could sleep through that racket.*

Monday's practice was easy. Several Raiders were nursing injuries, so Coach Smith focused on drills and formations, with a few "live" extra-point and field-goal attempts thrown in at the end.

Tuesday brought another scrimmage. Cody prepared for a long afternoon of spectating. He roamed the sideline, the desire for contact—for football eating at him like a physical hunger. The frustration was so great that he thought he might bite through his rubber mouth guard, which he had taken to chewing to ease the stress.

He glared at Coach Smith. *He's never gonna give me another chance,* Cody fumed. *We're supposed to forgive each other seventy times seven. I'd be happy for just once from him. But it's not gonna happen. Maybe I'll go out for cross-country next fall instead of football.*

He stopped thinking for a moment to watch Coach Smith, who had grabbed Terrance Dylan by the face mask, screaming at him, "If you don't learn the difference between a flag pattern and a post pattern, you're done playing wide receiver!"

Cody shook his head. Dylan was brand new to Grant this year. And he was a great player. He didn't deserve the treatment he was getting. Cody thought of one of his favorite Old Testament words—*smite.*

Smite Smith, he thought, smiling to himself. *That's what Dylan ought to do. I'd smite Smith if I were Dylan right now—especially if I had his biceps.*

The sound of Coach Smith's voice unsnapped Cody from his thoughts.

"Martin!" he spat. "Get over here!"

Cody felt his heart accelerate as he obeyed.

"Martin," Coach Smith said, without looking at him, "I'm gonna give you another chance to be a monster. But I mean just one more chance. You play tentatively out there, like your head's in the clouds—or somewhere else—and I'll bench you for the rest of the season. That is, if you don't get your head handed to you first. Football is a violent game, played by violent athletes, not philosophers and dreamers. Understand?"

Cody nodded as he saw his coach turn to him. "Good. Now, get in there for Betts. He's missed three straight tackles. At least I know you'll try to put a hit on somebody, not grope around like an old man looking for his glasses!"

Wow, Cody thought as he sprinted to the defensive huddle, *the way you've been treating me, Coach, that's almost a compliment!*

"Welcome back to the defense!" Pork Chop said, smiling, as Cody joined the huddle. "Let's show Coach Smith somethin'!"

Cody nodded. He thought of the damage he had done to the garage wall—the sense of power and relief it brought him. He couldn't smite Smith, but he vowed that someone was going to get rocked. As Bart

Evans called out his snap count, Cody's muscles tingled, as if electrically charged. Brett Evans went in motion, eventually coming set in the left slot between Paul Getman, the tight end, and Dylan, the other wide receiver.

"Slot left!" Cody barked, sliding into position in front of Brett. On the snap, Brett rocketed forward. Cody backpedaled, maintaining a two-yard cushion between himself and the lanky receiver. Ten yards into his pattern, Brett planted his left foot and cut toward the sideline.

A down-and-out, Cody thought. *Pretty crisp pattern, Brett, but I'm on it.*

Cody shot a glance into the backfield as he closed in on Brett. Bart cocked his arm and fired the pass, a near-perfect spiral. Brett was running out of field as he stretched for the pass, trying to reel in the ball and keep his feet in bounds at the same time.

As he prepared to slam into Brett, Cody saw that the ball was going to be off target. There was no way Brett could catch it unless he stepped out of bounds.

Cody didn't care. The pain of his mother's death, the humiliation of Coach Smith's taunts, the embarrassment of half a season on the bench—he loaded it all into one furious hit, which he unleashed on Brett Evans with a Neanderthal grunt.

He crashed into Brett's exposed left flank. The force of the impact drove the receiver into the bench along the sideline. He tumbled over the bench, a sprawling mess of arms and legs, before landing with a thud on his back. Bart Evans was the first one to his motionless brother's side. "He's out!" Cody heard him screaming, his voice quivering. "He's out cold! Somebody call 911!"

Panic flooded Cody's system. After making the hit, he had headed back to the field to collect praise from Pork Chop. But Chop sprinted right by him, toward the downed wideout.

Cody stood in the middle of the field, both hands clutching his face mask. "God, please forgive me," he whispered. "What have I done?"

"You stink, Martin!" Bart said, ripping off his helmet and marching toward midfield. "That was a cheap shot and you know it! This is just a scrimmage— what's wrong with you? If he's hurt bad, I'll see you after practice!"

"I'm sorry," Cody said quietly as he felt his head droop.

Cody watched as Bart returned to his brother's side. Half the team was crowded around the fallen receiver. Periodically, one of the Raiders would steal a glance over his shoulder at Cody, who stood frozen at midfield, alone like a leper.

Cody felt a wave of relief wash over him when, finally, Coach Smith helped Brett to a sitting position. Then Pork Chop, who was crouched in front of Brett, stood and offered his hand.

Brett pulled himself to his feet and stood blinking and slowly rotating his head. Cody felt himself drawn to his teammate, as if by magnetic force. He walked slowly but deliberately to Brett and extended his hand. "Brett, I'm sorry about the hit. You okay?"

Brett studied Cody's hand for a moment, then spat in it. "Yeah, I'm okay," he snapped, "no thanks to you! And you best watch yourself, Martin. You know what they say about paybacks!"

Brett wasn't at practice the following day. In the locker room, Coach Smith explained that he had suffered a slight concussion and wouldn't be in the lineup for that Saturday's game with West.

"Martin," Coach Smith said, "you played some at receiver last year, so you're gonna have to fill in. We'll have to make sure you get some reps with the first-team offense these next two days. We're gonna run through all pass plays at nine-tenths speed, so that should help prepare you for game conditions."

Cody looked up from lacing his shoes to see Bart glaring at him.

On the practice field, Cody was relieved to discover how easily the pass patterns came back to him. He ran deep posts, fly and flag routes, down-and-outs, down-and-ins, dig-and-gos, and comebacks.

He was able to get open consistently on Slaven, Brett's practice replacement at cornerback, but Bart didn't throw him one ball.

Cody was ready to complain to his QB, but Coach Smith beat him to it. "Bart," he snapped, "you have two wideouts, in case you've forgotten. Martin needs some touches, so you better throw him the ball, or I'll put Goddard in. For Pete's sake, quit being such a petty little baby!"

On the next play, Bart called a Red Basic, X-in, which called for Cody to run a down-and-in. Before he broke the huddle, Bart leaned toward Cody. "Go short, Martin," he said, "just about five yards before you make your cut. My arm's gettin' sore."

"Sure, Bart," Cody said, "no problem."

Cody took his place at wideout, standing parallel with the line of scrimmage, his hands ready at his sides. He made sure his shoulders were square, giving Slaven no hint of where the pattern was going.

As Bart called out the snap count, Cody fought back a smile. Slaven was giving him way too much cushion, a good seven yards. He would be wide open when he cut to the middle of the field.

He was off on the snap count. He sprinted forward, then cut sharply toward the middle. He knew he had Slaven beaten as he saw Bart cock his arm. The words "big gain" flashed in his mind as he prepared to receive the pass.

Cody knew Bart Evans had a strong arm, but he had no idea he could fire a ball so fast that it felt like it would imbed itself in his stomach. Through the pain and shock of a pass thrown twice as hard as needed, Cody tried to grab the ball as it rebounded off his mid-section, but it dribbled off his fingertips and dropped to the turf.

Cody wanted to fall to the ground too, but he braced his hands on his knees and fought for air. He felt tears stinging his eyes.

Bart waited for Cody to trot to the huddle and then unloaded on him: "Nice catch, butter-fingers! Man, Martin, that pass hit you right between the four and the one. What more do you want?"

There are about a hundred comebacks I'd like to throw in your face right now, Bart, he thought, *but there are also about a hundred proverbs about holding your tongue.*

So Cody said nothing. And he didn't receive another pass until Goddard came in to get a few reps with the first team.

Brett showed up to watch Friday's practice. When the team took a Gatorade break before working on kickoffs and kickoff returns, Cody seized the opportunity to apologize, again, to the injured receiver.

He saw Brett cross his arms as he approached. "Hey, Brett," he said, trying to sound cheerful and nonchalant, "it's good to see you. You feelin' okay?"

Brett rolled his eyes and then turned his back.

Cody stopped short, as if he'd run into a wall. He groped for something else to say, but came up with nothing that he could say to the back of Brett Evans' head.

Chapter 4
Fight or Forgive?

On Sunday morning, Blake pulled into the Martin driveway promptly at 10:30 to take Cody to church. Cody heard the beep of Blake's horn. He pushed himself away from the kitchen table, downed his half glass of orange juice in two gulps, and snatched his second Pop-Tart before heading for the door.

He was hoping Blake would ask him about the game so he could tell the tale of his first-ever middle-school touchdown pass reception. Sure it had been in a losing effort, and from the hand of Goddard, the backup QB, not Bart, the starter. But it was a sweet twelve-yard hook-and-go that made the difference between a 20-3 drubbing and a more respectable 20-10 defeat.

But the youth pastor had something else on his mind. Cody had barely buckled his seatbelt before the questioning began.

"Code," Blake said, "I want to follow up on something you said in my office a while back. I was reading through my notes last night, and it hit me."

Cody wrinkled his nose. "Good morning to you, too, B. And, may I ask, what hit you?"

Blake smiled anxiously. "Sorry to just dive right in, but we have a lot to talk about on the way to church. Anyway, you told me a while ago that you were feeling that something was incomplete—something was undone where your mom's concerned."

Cody stared at the half-eaten Pop-Tart in his hand. Suddenly his appetite had deserted him.

"Yeah, something is definitely not right. I mean, I'm finally playing ball like I should and that helps. You know, at the first football practice, Coach Smith told us to write down a goal for the season. I made one for the whole year. I wrote, 'This season is for my mom.' And you can't devote a year of sports to someone, then go out and play like a stiff. So I think I'm playing in a way that would make her proud, but I don't know."

They approached a red light, and Blake turned to look at him. "It seems to me you don't have peace about something."

Cody closed his eyes and searched his mind for answers. "I think maybe it's the funeral. It was a good service and all. It was cool when Pastor Taylor asked all the people to stand who Mom had helped in some way. Took them meals when they were sick. Watched their kids. Listened to their problems and gave them advice. Almost everybody in the whole church stood up. It made me so—I don't know—proud of her. I never realized how many people she reached out to."

Blake placed a hand on Cody's shoulder. "Your mom is a great example of how one person can touch hundreds of lives. And note what I said. *Is* a great example. Not was. The Bible says that the memory of the righteous will be a blessing. And the example set by a righteous person like your mom is one way that blessing shows itself."

Cody nodded slowly. "Yeah—you know, B, I think that might be kinda what my problem is. You see, when all of those people stood, I did too. But I'm her son. What else would you expect? I should have done more. I should have gone up there and said something. Before the funeral, Pastor Taylor said I was free to say a few words, but I knew I was too torn up inside. I woulda gotten up there and not been able to do anything but cry. I spent most of the service sobbing with my head in my hands as it was."

"Cody, nobody could expect a thirteen-year-old to speak at his own mother's memorial service."

"I know. But I wish I could have. I should have given her some kind of a tribute. I think that's what was missing—is missing. But I don't know what I can do now."

"Well—" Blake said. "What in the world!?"

Blake stomped his brake pedal, and he and Cody lurched forward against their seatbelts, before rocking back against their seats. The rail-thin runner who had bolted in front of Blake's car gave a helpless shrug, hurried from the middle of the street, and headed up the sidewalk.

"Drew Phelps." Blake chuckled. "He's gonna be a great runner someday—if he doesn't get himself killed."

Cody watched Drew float up the street, his feet barely kissing the ground. "Man, I wish I could run like that. They had a meet yesterday. He won."

"He should take a day off, enjoy the victory."

"I don't think he believes in the concept of a day off. Not even in the off-season. He works as hard as anybody I know. He hits the track and the roads as hard as Chop hits the weights."

Blake offered to take Cody to lunch after Sunday service, which Cody had tuned out of just after Pastor Taylor's opening joke. He had tried to concentrate on the sermon, but the images of Brett Evans spitting on him and turning his back on him loomed in his mind's eye, haunting him. He and the Evanses had been friends and teammates since Cody moved to Grant. Now, it seemed, that was over. Both twins were good athletes, so he was sure they would all continue to be teammates. But how could he play alongside two guys who hated him?

As he and Blake sat across from each other at Mamie's House o' Pies, Cody felt the youth pastor's eyes drilling into his skull. He shifted nervously on his side of the booth. "Do I have ketchup on my face or something?"

Blake smiled. "No, I was just wondering about a few things."

"Such as—"

"Such as where you were during the service today."

"What do you mean? I was there in the back row, like always. I didn't even sneak out for a donut."

"I mean, where your mind was."

"Oh. It was that obvious, huh?"

"I've seen horror-movie zombies with better powers of concentration."

"I'm sorry, B. I don't mean any disrespect to Pastor Taylor. I just can't get the thing with Brett off my mind."

"He's still holding a grudge, huh?"

"Like it was a bag of money."

"I'm sorry, Cody, I really am. It's hard when teammates can't get along."

Cody leaned back in the booth and smiled sadly. "Yeah, dude, I'll be glad when the season is over."

Blake nibbled on the end of his straw. "Don't be too glad. This Saturday is the final game of your middle-school career. Next year, you'll be playing with the big boys."

"Maybe."

Blake's eyes widened. "Maybe? What do you mean, maybe?"

Cody stirred his Coke with his straw, clinking the ice cubes against the side of his glass. He liked the sound. "If next year is anything like this year, maybe I'd be better off going out for cross-country. Drew says I should think about it."

"Nothing against cross-country, Code, but you're a football guy. How long have you been playing?"

"Since third grade."

"And you're ready to walk away from it now? Let me tell you from experience, high school football rocks! Those Friday-night games, under the lights, bleachers packed with parents and students—and big and little brothers and sisters. The energy, the competition, it's something you'll never forget. Every game I go to, I find myself wishing I could suit up and get out there one more time."

"Yeah, it is pretty cool. I've always gone to those games and dreamed what it would be like. It's like the big time, you know? But I don't know if I'm willing to go through this much garbage for even one more year. Besides, who knows if I'm even good enough to play high school ball?"

"I do."

"And you're an expert? I haven't seen you analyzing NFL games on ESPN."

"I'm not saying I'm an expert. But I know football. And I know a football player when I see one."

Cody shook his head sadly. "I don't know if I'm a football player anymore. I don't know what I am."

Cody was silent on the drive home. He tried to picture himself in a blue and silver Grant High School uniform. Even only a year away from ninth grade, high school seemed like another world. And high school football? That was another planet. Cody thought of 220-pound Doug Porter charging through the line on a fullback off-tackle. Could he ever hope to bring down someone as big and powerful as Pork Chop's brother?

He wondered if God would punish him for not paying attention in church. *I didn't just disrespect Pastor Taylor*, he thought, *I disrespected God. It would have been better if I'd just stayed home.*

He looked out the window and realized where he was. "Stop the car!" he blurted.

Blake looked around frantically as he braked. "What? Do you see Drew again?"

"No. It's not that. I just need to get out here. You can go ahead and head home."

"Why?"

Cody grabbed the door handle. "There's something I gotta do. I just realized it."

"What do you have to do?"

Cody gave a cryptic smile. "Matthew 5:23 and 24."

Blake shrugged. "I'm drawing a blank on that."

"Come on, dude," Cody called over his shoulder as he began jogging down Vindicator Avenue. "You're the one who taught it to me."

Cody stood on the Evanses' doorstep. He could hear the muffled sound of an NFL game. The Jets versus somebody. Miami maybe. Cody whispered to himself, "'Therefore, if you are offering your gift at the altar and there remember that your brother has something against you, leave your gift there in front of the altar. First go and be reconciled to your brother; then come and offer your gift.'" Cody paused. "Well, I didn't remember before I went to the 'altar,' but I think this is better than nothing."

Drawing in a deep breath, he jabbed the doorbell with his right index finger.

So this is what Brett and Bart are gonna look like when they're adults, Cody thought when Mr. Evans opened the door. *Kinda wrinkly. I wonder if they're gonna be bald like he is.*

Mr. Evans stood before him, shirtless and unshaven, holding the screen door open with his shoulder. Cody extended his hand, just as his mother had taught him. "Hello, sir, I'm Cody Martin, and I—"

"I know who you are," Mr. Evans said impatiently. "You got a lot of nerve if you're here trying to sell me something. We don't need no candy bars. We don't need no stinkin' magazines. Especially not from you."

"No, sir, I'm not selling anything. I would just like to talk to Brett, please."

Mr. Evans snorted. "What makes you think he wants to talk to you?"

Cody could feel his will melting. Something in him wanted to leap off the porch and sprint all the way home. But he forced himself to tilt his chin and look at Brett's father.

"Sir," he said, trying to keep his voice calm and even, "if Brett could come to the door for just a second, I have something important to talk with him about."

Mr. Evans turned without speaking and disappeared from Cody's view. "Brett!" he heard moments later, "Cody Martin is at the door."

Cody didn't like the way Mr. Evans said his name. He used the same singsongy nasal voice the eighth graders had favored two years ago, when they taunted Cody and his sixth grade classmates during their first weeks of middle school.

"Yeah?" Brett Evans said, glaring at Cody through the closed screen door.

Cody felt his cheeks growing hot, like when he opened the oven to check on his TV dinners. "Hey, Brett. You up for a walk around the block or something? I'd like to talk with you."

"You gonna get me away from my house so you can take another cheap shot at me? Maybe I'll be the one handin' out the shots."

Cody pushed down the response that was fighting to escape his mouth: *It wasn't a cheap shot, Brett. It was a clean hit. Hard, but clean. If you can't take the contact, don't play football. For cryin' out loud—quit being such a baby!*

Then, after a quick prayer for self-control, he said, "I'm sorry about the hit. I really am. Brett, please, can we just take a quick walk?"

Brett stared at him warily. "Okay," he said after several seconds, "whatever." He pushed the screen door open and let it bang shut behind him. Then he marched down the driveway without checking to see if Cody was following him. At the end of the block, Brett turned abruptly. "This is as far as I go, Martin," he said. "You got something to say, you better say it here. Now."

Cody looked to the sky, hoping earnestly to draw divine strength from above. "Brett, I've said I'm sorry a bunch of times already," he began, "and I'll say it a hundred more times if that's what it takes to make it right with you. I wish you hadn't gotten hurt, and I'd take the hit back if I could."

Brett's eyes narrowed to a slit. "Well," he said icily, "you can't."

"I know," Cody sighed. "I just want you to know it wasn't intentional. C'mon man, you know I don't roll like that."

"I don't know what to think about you anymore, Martin."

Cody forced himself to look Brett in the eyes. "Look, maybe I can explain. I'm not going to make excuses, but I'm hoping when I tell you a couple of things, you'll stop hating me."

"Well, I don't have all day."

"Okay, here's the deal. It's been hard dealing with my mom's dying. Sometimes I want to play so hard, to make her proud. But other times, this—I don't know— sadness starts to, like, cover me up. I feel like it's going to suffocate me. It can happen anytime. Even in a game. So, earlier this season, I lost my concentration a few times. And I played like crap because of it. I got rocked by blockers I shoulda seen coming. I missed tackles. I jumped off-sides. I misread plays. You name it."

Brett nodded slowly. "And you got in Coach Smith's doghouse."

"Big time."

Brett wagged his head slowly. "Coach Smith holds grudges, you know. Both my older brothers told me that. He's kind of a psycho that way. He doesn't forget stuff."

"I don't know about all that, Brett. All I know is that he started treating me like something he stepped in. And I was desperate to get on his good side again. And I had all this anger in me, too. Because he was callin' me names, holding me out of games, telling me, 'You're weak and soft, Martin! Why don't you go play on the swing set!'"

"I know. I heard."

"Anyway, there was like this pressure building up inside of me, and that day at practice, I just felt like, if I didn't hit someone or something, I was gonna explode. And then I was covering you on that one play—and I just lost it. That was wrong. And I'm so sorry."

Brett started walking back toward his house. Cody walked by his side, trying to gauge his mood.

When he got back to his doorstep, Brett paused. "Well, thanks, I guess, for coming over. I know it must be hard on you. I can't even imagine what it would be like, if—"

"I hope you don't ever have to find out."

"Yeah, me, too. Anyway, apology accepted, I guess. I'm not gonna be like Coach Smith."

"You gonna be able to play the last game?"

"Yeah. Our doctor said it's okay. My head hurt for a day or two. But I'm fine now."

"Good. I'm glad. If you want, I'll ask Coach Smith to put you back at starting receiver."

"I don't know about that. Just do what you think you have to do, I guess. Look, I gotta get inside. Homework, you know."

"Okay, Brett. Thanks."

Cody could hardly wait to call Blake and tell him the news.

"I'm proud of you for not giving up with Brett," Blake said, his sincerity evident, even over the phone. "You may not see it yet, but your efforts to make things right will make a huge impact on him. And I admire your long-suffering with Coach Smith this year."

Cody sighed. "Well, you got the suffering part right."

"I'm sure it hasn't been easy, Code. But you didn't quit. That shows me something. It shows Coach Smith something, too. Now, just finish strong this weekend. And next season will be better. I have a feeling."

"Yeah, who knows? Maybe I'll make the JV team. Doug says Chop will make varsity lineman. He might even start. I'll be glad for him, but I'll miss playing behind him."

"Um-hmm," Blake said.

"You know, during games, Chop keeps talking to me when we're on defense. He smacks me on the helmet and says, 'You got my back, right, Code?' Like he needs anyone to watch his back."

Blake frowned thoughtfully. "I don't know, Code. We all need someone to back us up sometime. Even the biggest and strongest—and cockiest—of us."

"You think?"

"I know. Now get offa my phone line. I got things to do."

"You mean like take a nap?"

"No comment."

Cody watched the Broncos battle the Raiders on TV. Midway through the fourth quarter, grogginess spread through him like smoke. He stood up and paced in front of the TV set to keep himself awake. When the Broncos finally won the game on a last-second field goal, he flopped onto the living room couch.

When he woke, he blinked his eyes, straining to focus at the liquid-crystal digits on his watch. It was two minutes after seven, and his dad still wasn't home from the office.

"Working all day on a Sunday," Cody muttered as he padded to the kitchen to make dinner for himself. "Mom woulda never stood for that."

On Monday, as the team dressed for practice, Cody shot a glance at the locker room chalkboard, which typically bore an inspirational quote from Knute Rockne, Vince Lombardi, or Dick Butkus. Occasionally the board displayed more practical information, such as special instructions for the day's practice or a diagram of a new offensive formation.

Today, however, the only thing on the board was a large, blocky number "1," shaded around the edges to make it look three-dimensional.

"Coach Smith must have forced an art student to do that," Pork Chop said, as he arrived at Cody's side, the two of them staring at the chalkboard as if it were a painting in an art gallery.

"Yeah, you're right," Cody said. "He can't even draw a straight line or make a circle that doesn't look like an amoeba."

Coach Smith explained the mystery of the "1" before calisthenics and stretching. "Fellas," he began, "I hope you all saw what was on the board in the locker room today."

He paused, noting thirty-two bobbing heads, before continuing. "That number is gonna be up all week. And there's a reason for it. Now I know we aren't number one in our conference. We're not ranked first in any statistical category, team or individual."

"I'd be first in tackles if I didn't get double-teamed on every play," Pork Chop whispered to Cody.

"Anyway," Coach Smith said, "here's what the '1' is all about: Our final game of the year is five days away—against the undefeated number-one team in the league. In fact, East is probably the best eighth grade team in the whole state. I hear that Bobby Cabrera has gained at least 100 yards rushing in every game."

Coach Smith was pacing now, speaking slowly and deliberately. It looked to Cody like he had rehearsed this speech, but was now struggling to remember it correctly. "Now I'm not saying we can beat East," the coach said, smacking a thick fist into the palm of his other hand. "But we can give them—and everybody in the stands—something to remember. We can go out and finish the season with a game we can all be proud of. What I'm tryin' to say is, we're not number one, but let's go out and play one game like we are! Whaddya say?"

The Raiders roared their approval and began practice with a fury that would carry them through the week. In fact, Coach Smith had to cut short Wednesday's scrimmage after Betts and Goddard were shaken up on consecutive plays.

"You guys are hittin' like men, and I'm proud of ya," Coach Smith said, his voice ragged from three days of yelling. "But we gotta make sure we save some of this fire for East. Besides, I'm afraid that

Porter is going to put somebody in the hospital if we don't get him off the field."

Cody was the last player out of the showers after practice. And he deliberately dressed slower than his teammates so that he could be alone in the locker room. He sat on the wooden bench in front of his locker, his helmet on his lap.

He ran his fingers over the plastic crown of his helmet, feeling every scratch, gouge, and ding. He smiled. Given the amount of time he had spent standing on the sidelines during mid-season, his "hat," as Coach Smith called it, carried a respectable number of battle scars.

Cody noted the maroon smear near the left ear hole. That was from the Central game, probably the doing of Tucker. The divot on top of the helmet was from Holy Family and a head-on collision with Mack. The black smudges on the back must have been from one of the times he had been kicked or stepped on in a pileup.

He set the helmet on the bench next to him. Coach had said Mike Singletary broke sixteen helmets in four years at Baylor—all of them his own. Cody shook his head in admiration.

I'm no Singletary, he thought, *but, still, this hat has seen some action. And on Saturday, I'm collecting some green paint, Cabrera's, I hope.*

During the remaining two days leading up to the season finale, the fever that began in the Raider locker room spread through the whole school. Posters lined the hallways, bearing proclamations such as GROUND THE EAGLES! PLUCK THE EAGLES! RAIDERS FINISH STRONG! And EAGLES: UNBEATEN NO MORE!

In a pep assembly Friday morning, Coach Smith stood in the red circle in the middle of the basketball court, holding a microphone like it was a dead fish. He shifted his weight from left foot to right, like a rhythmless man trying to dance for the first time.

"Uh," he said, pausing to dab his moist forehead with a handkerchief, "this is a big game for us tomorrow. And, uh, we would appreciate your support. Please show up tomorrow. In full force!"

The students filling the bleachers roared their approval. As if energized by their support, Coach Smith threw his fist in the air, which raised the noise level even more.

As one of the team captains, Pork Chop got his chance with the mike, too, and he handled it like a seasoned game show host.

"Coach is right," he began, nodding deferentially at Coach Smith. "This is a huge game for us. In fact, it's the biggest of our lives. So, if you don't come tomorrow and scream your heads off for us, I'm gonna eat all your lunches on Monday!"

A burst of laughter and applause erupted from the stands. Pork Chop basked in the admiration for a moment, then raised both hands and began lowering them slowly, as if conducting an orchestra. When the throng was quiet again, Chop brought the mike to his mouth.

"One more thing," he announced, "all you students, as you know, get in to our games for free. Well, you better enjoy it while you can. Because someday, when I'm playing for the Broncos, you're gonna have to pay big bucks to see me in action!"

The students cheered again before breaking into unison chants of "Chop! Chop! Chop!"

Before practice that afternoon, Cody found himself next to Pork Chop in the locker room.

"Hey, Chop," he said, "great speech this morning, but I have a question. How many school lunches do you think you could eat, without throwing up, I mean."

Pork Chop shook his head in mock disappointment. "Code," he said, "I wasn't threatening to eat anybody's lunch literally. It was just a figure of speech. C'mon, dude, catch up. If you're gonna be my best friend, you're gonna have to work to stay with me intellectually."

With that, Chop belched contentedly and walked to his locker, his rubber cleats clicking like tap shoes across the hard floor.

Friday's practice was designed to be easy, to conserve players' energy and avoid injuries. But Pork Chop twisted his ankle during agility drills and got into a shoving match with Berringer over the ownership of a cup of Gatorade.

After the final practice ended, Cody and Pork Chop walked to the locker room together. "So, Chop," Cody said, "you think we have any chance against East?"

Pork Chop stepped carefully from the field to the cracking asphalt of the parking lot, apparently favoring his tender ankle. "I don't know, Code. It's hard to imagine how good they must be. I mean, they handled Central twenty-zip. They pitched a shutout on a team that smoked us. It's scary."

Cody whistled through his teeth. "You're scared? You didn't sound that way at the pep rally."

Pork Chop muttered something Cody couldn't decipher.

"Huh?"

"Nothing, Code. Look, I'm not scared. I'm just sayin' . . . it's been a long season. I'm tired. I'm hurting. And I'm sick of Berringer and his big mouth. Don't get me wrong. I'm bringing the war for thirty-two minutes tomorrow. It's just that—I don't know. I guess I'll be glad when the season's over."

Cody slapped his hand on Chop's left shoulder pad. "Come on, Chop. You've had a great season. It's not your fault we're not very good this year. But it's just one game—let's go for it. Let's hang a loss on those hot dogs. Wouldn't that be cool?"

"Yeah, it would. But I don't know."

"Come on, Chop. If you get fired up, most of the other guys will too. You're our captain."

"Yeah, but a good captain wouldn't lie to his troops."

"You really think we have no chance? I can't believe what I'm hearin'."

"I'm not saying there is no chance. There's always a chance. That's why they play the game."

"Well, that's what you need to show to the team. Hope. Because if you don't have it, nobody's going to have it."

Pork Chop arched one eyebrow. "Not even you?"

Cody fixed his eyes on the horizon. "I don't know, Chop. It's my final junior high game. My dad's going to be there—I hope. I'm gonna go big, no matter what."

Pork Chop smiled. "You know what? Then I will, too. You just inspired me."

Cody felt his mouth drop open. "I inspired you?"

"Hey, I'm not ashamed to admit it. You're a church boy. You know that David was badder than Goliath. I guess I should tell you, since you obviously aren't perceptive enough to realize it, but it's good for me to know you've got my back. Out on the field and everywhere, you know?"

"Yeah?"

"Yeah. It wasn't the same playin' on the D-line without you out there, backing me up. Because I know if a ball carrier is lucky and gets by me, you've got my back. That's why I'm not afraid to battle two blockers, even three. 'Cuz I know you're behind me and you won't let me down."

Cody walked several steps in stunned silence.

Pork Chop smiled knowingly. "What, I rock your world or something by admitting I'm not Superman and I can use a little help now and then?"

"Yeah," Cody answered after a thoughtful pause. "I guess you did."

-||||||-

Glancing at his watch, Cody noted it was 9 p.m. He wanted to go to bed early, as he always tried to do the night before a game.

"Come on, Dad," he whispered, "where are you? We need to talk."

He woke to the sensation of his dad gently tugging on his arm. "Code," he said in a half-whisper, "why don't you head up to bed? Guess you fell asleep on the couch, huh?"

Cody blinked and tried to focus on his father's face. "I . . . I guess so. Is it really after ten?"

His dad nodded.

"Hey, Dad, before I go up, I have a question, kind of."

Cody's dad sighed loudly. "Please don't pester me about going to church again. I've told you over and over, I'll go when I am ready. And I'm not ready yet!"

Cody swallowed hard. "No, it's not about that, Dad. I mean, I do wish you would start going with me again—but, uh, what I was going to say is that tomorrow is the final game of the season. The final game of my middle school career."

"Wow, Code, the season sure went by fast."

Cody yawned. "I guess so. Anyway, I guess I understand why you haven't been able to make it to any of the games this year, but tomorrow, it's important, you know. You think you can make it, just this once?"

"Sure, son. I'll be there. I have to go into the office again in the morning, but I'll come to the stadium right from work. What time is the game?"

"Two o'clock, just like all the Saturday games. So, you'll be there? You promise?"

"I promise."

On game day, Cody walked to school after eating a lunch of microwaveable chicken noodle soup, followed by two peanut butter sandwiches. He reached the school at 12:30. The East bus hadn't even arrived in the parking lot. Entering the locker room moments later, he saw Coach Smith seated on a bench at the far end. A feeling of uneasiness swept over him and he backed away, hoping to exit unseen.

But Coach Smith saw him before he took three steps. "Hey, Martin," he said. His voice was tired.

Cody walked slowly toward his coach. As he drew near, he saw that the man's eyes were red and weary.

Maybe he's allergic to something, Cody thought. *Hope it isn't me.*

"Sit down, Martin."

It sounded more like a suggestion than a command.

"You ready for today, Martin?"

"Yes, sir, Coach. I'm going to give it everything I have. We all are. We're going to play hard for you."

"Thanks, Martin."

Coach Smith began massaging his temples with his stubby fingers.

"Coach," Cody asked tentatively, "are you okay?"

"Yeah, sure," he answered absently. "It's just been a long season. A disappointing one."

"Yeah, I think I know what you mean."

"I'll be honest with you, Martin," Coach Smith said, interrupting himself with a long sigh, "your class is the best crop of athletes this school has had in a long time. Then Alston decides not to play football. Doesn't want to mess up that pretty face or whatever. Berringer has an off year. Can't grasp the concept of running around defenders, not into them. I get out-coached half the time. I try to put in these trick plays to confuse the opposition, and the only person I confuse is myself—and my own team."

"Yeah," Cody said, trying to inject maturity into his voice, "it's been a tough season all the way around."

"You ain't lyin', Martin. You know, I've been here eight years and never won a league championship. Not even when Doug Porter was here, and he's the best I've ever seen. Hands down. We were six and zero when he was in eighth grade and then he gets his hand stepped on and broken. We lose our last two games and finish second."

Cody nodded and said the only word that entered his mind, "Bummer."

Coach Smith stood. "Anyway, that's enough groaning and moaning from me. We better both start getting our game faces on. Who knows, Martin, maybe today we'll go out with a bang."

"Like I said, we're gonna play hard for you, Coach," Cody said sincerely.

"I know. Thanks."

As Cody dressed out, players began to trickle into the locker room. He smiled when he saw the Evans twins. Brett nodded at him, but when Bart's eyes lit on Cody, he quickly looked away.

Pork Chop came in behind Betts, headphones on and rapping along with a hip-hop song Cody recognized but couldn't identify by title.

Once Chop was in his game pants, cleats, and gray undershirt, he put his Discman in his locker and began working the room, circulating among his teammates.

"Cabrera is a fast little dude," Cody heard him tell Berringer. "But so are you. Don't let him get behind you on pass patterns. And don't let him get up a head of steam in the open field."

Then it was on to Matt Slaven, who played next to Chop on the offensive line. "We give up no sacks today, big Matt. Bart gets all day to throw. And when we run, we're gonna blast holes so big you can march elephants through them. Sideways."

Cody smiled. *This is the guy who, just yesterday, thought we were gonna get stomped?*

Coach Smith's pregame pep talk was short. "This whole season has been mediocre," he began. "You haven't always played well."

Cody, who was staring at the circular drain in the middle of the locker room floor, looked up when Coach Smith stopped talking. He saw the coach looking at him. "And I," Coach Smith said, "sometimes haven't coached well. And maybe I've been a little hard on some of you.

"But that is all behind us. In front of us is one more game. Your last game in a Grant uniform. For some of you, this will be your last real football game. East is undefeated. They killed Central, and Central killed us. I'm not saying we can beat them. We probably can't. But we can go out with an effort we can all be proud of. An effort your parents and your school can be proud of."

Coach Smith gave the whole speech without changing his tone. He wouldn't get much of a grade in Speech & Communications, Cody thought. But he spoke the truth.

Then the coach turned to the chalkboard and began to write, his chalk stick scuffing and scratching against the slate surface. When he was finished, he set down the chalk and brushed his hands together briskly. Chalk dust floated in the air in front of him, the effect reminding Cody of the smoke machines used to add drama to a rock star's or professional wrestler's big entrance.

When the dust had settled to the floor, Coach Smith stepped to the side of the board, admiring his work, as if he'd just painted the Mona Lisa. But he had crafted only words, not pictures.

Cody recognized the verse immediately, "The battle is not always to the strong, nor the race to the swift. But time and chance happen to them all."

Pork Chop leaned toward Cody and whispered, his breath heavy with the aroma of bologna and mustard. "That's from your favorite book, isn't it, dude?"

Cody nodded.

Pork Chop stood and slapped Cody across the back. "My man here says those words are from the Bible, so I say it's time to get out there and give East a whuppin' of biblical contortions!"

"You heard the man!" Coach Smith chimed in. The team sprang to their feet and cheered. "Apparently," Cody hollered to his best friend as he joined the mass of jumping and whooping humanity in the middle of the locker room, "nobody even cares that you said biblical 'contortions,' instead of 'proportions.'"

Pork Chop smiled. "You weren't listening. I said we're gonna give them contortions of biblical proportions!"

Chapter 5

In the Eagles' Talons?

With the crowd on its feet, stomping and cheering, the Raiders received the opening kickoff from East. Berringer secured the pigskin at his own fifteen and bolted eighteen yards up the center of the field before running into a green wall of defenders.

Three handoffs—all to Berringer—later, Grant had gained only seven yards and was forced to punt.

After a fair catch of the punt, East began operations from its own thirty. The Eagles went for a quick TD on first down, but Nottingham, their QB, overthrew Cabrera by five yards. Cody whistled through his teeth as he saw the ball sail well beyond Cabrera's outstretched hands.

My man, he scolded himself angrily, thumping himself on the chest. *And he had a step on me. That coulda been trouble. No way do I catch Cabrera from behind.*

As he jogged back to the line of scrimmage, Cody had an additional thought, *Hmm, if old Solomon were watching this game, I bet he'd tell me, "See what I mean about the race not always being to the swift?"*

On second and ten, East sent Williams, their full-back, into the center of the Grant defense. Pork Chop was the center of the Grant defense. Third and ten.

"They're gonna pass," Pork Chop told his team-mates in the ensuing defensive huddle. "DBs and 'backers, be ready." Then he winked at Cody. "Monsters, too. They double-teamed me that first pass. They'll probably do it again, so that's gonna create a gap for somebody. And if it doesn't, that's okay. Because they can block me, but I won't stay blocked!"

On the third-down snap, both of East's wideouts went long. Landers, the tight end, ran a down-and-in, with Cody on him like a shadow. Cody stole a glance into the East backfield. Nottingham was scrambling to his right, Pork Chop in furious pursuit. Landers broke from his pattern and sprinted downfield. The move caught Cody by surprise, and he dashed to make up the five-yard cushion Landers had put between the two of them.

Cody scanned the backfield again as he closed in. Near the sideline now, Nottingham hurled the ball in Landers's general direction. But he was off balance and panicked when he threw, thanks to Pork Chop, and the ball floated, not zipped, toward its target. That gave Cody time to move alongside Landers, who then changed direction and tried to run under the rainbow of a pass. Cody noted the receiver's eyes as he moved with him. He saw them widen. Then, predictably, Landers's arms came up to receive the pass.

Reacting to the tell-tale signals, Cody shot both his arms up too, as if Mr. Dawson had just asked the class a history question, and for once, Cody Martin knew the answer and was desperate to get his teacher's attention.

Cody turned his head just in time to see the ball and deflect it with his right hand. He sighed audibly as the pigskin bounced harmlessly to the ground.

As Cody trotted back to the line of scrimmage, Pork Chop intercepted him and head-butted him so hard that he saw tiny fireworks popping before his eyes.

"That's what I call pass defense, Crash!" Chop gushed. "That's the way to read a receiver. Oh, baby, that was shades of Neon Deion on ESPN Classic. That was prime time, baby!"

Smiling, Cody scanned the bleachers, searching for his dad. He saw Blake, sitting between Robyn and Doug and Mr. Porter, but Luke Martin wasn't among them. *Maybe he's just running a bit late*, Cody thought hopefully.

Back on the field, the Raider offense couldn't build momentum from the defense's stellar play. Bart overthrew his brother twice, and Berringer could manage only six hard-fought yards on a run off tackle. Cody sat out the entire offensive series, hopeful that he would get back in the action next time the Raiders had the ball. Coach Smith usually used his receivers to shuttle in plays, but on this series, he resorted to signaling them in from the sidelines.

Goddard got off a decent punt, and East took over at its own twenty-six. Cody watched in near disbelief as the Eagles ran Cabrera three times up the middle. Each time, Pork Chop smothered him like a huge grandma welcoming her five-year-old grandchild.

The first quarter ended as the East punter shanked one off his foot. It would be first and ten for Grant at midfield.

Between quarters, Coach Smith quickly gathered his team on the sideline. "Fellas," he said, "we're winning."

Betts and several other players whipped their heads around toward the scoreboard, which stood behind the south end zone. It read, Grant–0, Guest–0.

Reading the minds of his players, Coach Smith

chuckled. "No, guys, you didn't miss a touchdown or anything. I'm talking about winning the war of field position. Every time they get the ball, they're deeper in their own end. And look at where we are now. Halfway to pay dirt. Listen to me—we can win this thing. An hour ago, I wasn't sure. But now I can feel it. Let's take advantage of where we are. First offense back on the field. Now!"

On first down, Berringer scooted around the left end for seven yards. Brett Evans sprinted in from the sidelines, bearing Coach Smith's play for second and three—a three-step drop by Bart, then a quick-out pass to his twin.

As the play developed, Brett was blanketed by an East cornerback. Bart tried to force the ball to him anyway. If the corner had possessed better hands, it would have been an interception. Grant was lucky to come out of the play with a third and still three yards to go.

In the huddle, Brett looked at his brother and shrugged, his palms to the sky. Seizing the opportunity, Pork Chop interjected, "Martin was wide open, Bart. I saw him after I pancaked their tackle. C'mon, man, don't force 'em like that, or you're gonna get picked. You're lucky that DB has hands of stone."

Then Pork Chop looked to Brett, who nodded in agreement.

"Just do your job, Porter," Bart muttered, "and let me do mine."

Dylan shuttled in the next play, sending Brett sprinting for the sideline. Cody felt a jolt of excitement when he heard the plan—an eight-yard hook route for him. As the center hiked the ball, Cody blasted from the line of scrimmage, as if going out for a long bomb. But once he saw he was past the first-down marker, he stopped short and hooked his body back toward the line of scrimmage.

Bart's pass was a burner—low and hard. Cody bent at the knees and drew himself downward. He placed his hands together, palms up and fingers spread wide, forming a flesh-and-bones football-sized basket. He could feel blades of grass tickling the backs of his hands as he scooped the ball into his gut.

As he clutched the ball close to his body, he braced himself for the impact, which came almost immediately. The East corner hit him high on his back, and his shoulder pads absorbed the blow. Cody was driven face-first into the turf, but he popped up like a piece of toast and handed the ball to the nearest referee. He smiled as he saw the first down chain move.

Grant earned another first down on a twelve-yard QB scramble around the right end. Brett, back in the game, threw a vicious block to spring his brother. The

Raiders had marched to the East twenty-nine, their deepest penetration of the game. Coach Smith signaled the play in from the sideline this time. Cody nodded as he processed the signals.

This could work, he thought.

Cody and Brett manned the two wideout positions, bookending the offensive line. Cody studied his defender, who was playing only two yards off of him.

Go ahead and get right up in my face, dude, Cody thought. *If I can get by you on this slant route, you're toast. And I think I can outrun your safety.*

He stole a quick glance toward the stands. He thought he might have caught a glimpse of his dad, next to Robyn, but he couldn't be sure. And there was no time for another look because the center had snapped the ball.

Cody took two deliberate strides toward the sideline, then ricocheted back to the middle of the field, at a crisp 45-degree angle.

The corner had bitten on the fake to the outside and was now scrambling to atone for his mistake. But he was too late. Bart's pass was near perfect, nestling into Cody's waiting hands at the twenty-two.

As Cody angled his way toward the end zone, he saw the safety, who was pursuing him, stumble and tumble to the ground.

Pay dirt, here I come, Cody thought gleefully, as he crossed the fifteen.

"Clear sailing, Code," called a voice behind him.

Cody whipped his head around and saw Brett trailing him by about three yards, escorting him to the end zone.

"Brett," he said breathlessly, as he crossed the ten, "heads up!"

Making sure he had eye contact with his teammate, Cody carefully lobbed the ball to him.

Brett bobbled the lateral momentarily, and Cody felt panic clutch his heart like a cold hand. But, as he reached the five, Brett gained control of the oval and secured it into his gut as he sprinted into the end zone.

Cody waited for Brett to toss the ball to the referee, then chest-bumped his fellow wide receiver. Seconds later, Bart sprinted into the end zone, bear-hugged his brother and hoisted him off his feet.

Goddard booted the extra point, and the East Eagles trailed in a game for the first time in almost two years.

Brett found a place beside Cody on the sideline, and they watched the ensuing kickoff together. "Code," he said, as the ball blew off the tee and Goddard had to re-set it, "thanks, man. You didn't have to do that. But I'm glad you did. You know, that was my first real touchdown. Ever."

Cody turned to Brett. "Really?"

Brett nodded. "Really. Never had one in Bantams. And not even in Mighty Mites. And what's cool is that my whole family got to see it. Even my big brothers are here. So, like I said, thanks."

"Brett," Cody said tentatively, after Goddard finally got his kick away and Cabrera returned it to his own twenty-seven, "don't thank me." He pointed to the sky. "Thank him."

The two receivers stood in awkward silence for a moment. *I hope I didn't freak him out,* Cody thought. *But, oh well. I'm glad I said it. I know who deserves the credit for what I did. It sure wasn't my idea.*

Bart Evans interrupted Cody's self-reflection with a playful slap on the helmet. "Martin," he said, "what you did out there, that was classy. I don't know too many guys who would give up a TD like that. You didn't have to do it, but I'm glad you did."

"I know I didn't have to," Cody said. "But I needed to. So, we're cool now?"

Bart let a smile stretch across his face. "Oh, yeah," he said, "we're more than cool. And if we win this game, we'll be subzero!"

East couldn't answer Grant's score. On third and ten, Pork Chop erupted up the middle and sacked Nottingham at the twenty.

Dylan fair-caught the ensuing punt at the Grant forty-five, and the Raiders looked to pad their lead, fearing that a mere touchdown advantage wouldn't hold up against East.

Coach Smith called Dylan's number on a fly pattern. A strong runner, Dylan got behind the Eagle defense, and it looked like another touchdown pass for Bart. But in his eagerness to get the pass off, the Grant QB threw a knuckleball that helicoptered only twenty yards, fluttering into the eager arms of Cabrera, whom the East coach had inserted at cornerback to bolster the team's pass defense. Cabrera returned the interception all the way to the Grant thirty before a frustrated Bart leaped on his back and rode him to the ground.

Nottingham gained six yards on a first down quarterback draw, and Cody was certain he could feel the energy and momentum draining from his team. As the defense huddled, his eyes met Pork Chop's, and they nodded almost simultaneously. Cody wondered how many times during their long friendship it had happened. More times, he was sure, than he had fingers and toes.

"Okay," Chop said, smacking his fist into his palm, "it's time to bring the war. It's time for jailbreak!"

"You sure, Chop?" Brett countered. "An all-out blitz—that's kinda risky. We gotta protect our lead."

"Look," Pork Chop said evenly, "we're not gonna protect anything. This is our game. We gotta go out and grab it." He turned his attention to Cody. "Co," he said, "I'm gonna take my blockers inside. You should be able to shoot off my left hip. Get the sack! We need it!"

Cody felt his muscles tingling as he took his place behind the D-line. "Monster left," he called. His eyes locked on Pork Chop's ample backside. He was ready to rip through the path his friend would no doubt clear.

Then he turned his attention to the ball, resting under the center's hands. That was his cue. He would block out the cadence of the snap count. It was all about the ball. As soon as that brown oval moved, even twitched, he would be off, like a sprinter exploding from the starting blocks.

Don't look away, even for a second. Don't even blink, he ordered himself.

Five seconds later, Cody was grateful for his keen concentration. As soon as Nottingham moved in behind the center, the snap came immediately, before a word from the QB. East had hoped to catch Grant unaware, but Cody was ready.

And, true to his word, Pork Chop herded the East guard and center to their left, giving Cody a clear lane to the QB, who had taken only two steps back from center when Cody slammed into him, toppling him easily.

Pork Chop pointed at Cody as he got up from his fourth sack of the season. Cody smiled and pointed right back.

Grant took over after a punt and played it safe—and went into halftime with a 7-0 lead.

The two teams walked to their respective end zones to spend the ten-minute halftime regrouping and rehydrating.

Cody slid his helmet off his head. His hair felt wet and sticky against his skin. He gulped in deep breaths of the crisp autumn air before heading to the Gatorade cooler.

Coach Smith removed his baseball cap and cleared his throat. "We're halfway to the biggest upset in school history," he announced. "But only halfway. We have our foot on their throat, and we can't let 'em up. That team over there has pride. They haven't lost all season, and they sure as shootin' haven't been shut out. They're gonna fight like wildcats until the final tick of the clock. So we have to be ready. We have to be tough. Boys, you played an outstanding half of football. You do that for sixteen more minutes, and you'll earn a victory that you'll remember. Always."

"Speaking of remember always," Pork Chop whispered conspiratorially to Cody, "check out who's leaning over the fence behind our bench."

Cody looked over and saw his dad, his long arms dangling over the fence that circled the field. He was pointing at his watch and shrugging apologetically. Cody smiled and gave him the okay sign. His dad wiped his forehead in a sign of relief and then pounded his fist against his heart.

Cody felt the weight of Pork Chop's hand on his shoulder pad. "We're gonna make your pops proud, dude. Your mom, too."

Cody nodded and put on his helmet.

East stumbled on its first second-half opportunity, collecting penalties for holding, illegal motion, and offensive pass interference on three consecutive plays.

"They're rattled," Pork Chop said to Cody. "We've rented space inside their heads, and they're gettin' desperate."

Grant couldn't move the ball either, but a booming punt from Goddard sailed over Cabrera's head and rolled to a stop on the Eagle nine.

East picked up two first downs, one courtesy of a roughing-the-passer call on Pork Chop, but their mini-drive ultimately stalled at their own twenty-eight.

Only a slip in the open field kept Berringer from taking the ensuing punt all the way to the end zone, but Grant still took over at its own forty-two. After a counterplay by Berringer gained six yards on first down, Coach Smith sent in a play he had called only once before all season—an end around to the wide receiver. Cody, in this case.

Cody nervously flexed his fingers in the huddle. *Don't fumble. Don't fumble. Don't fumble,* he admonished himself. *And by the way, don't fumble!*

On Bart's third sharp staccato "Hut!" Cody took one step forward, as if to begin a pass pattern or blocking assignment and then wheeled around to his left. He passed behind Bart, who slammed the ball hard into his stomach.

Then the Grant QB pivoted back toward the line of scrimmage and blocked a charging East linebacker, sealing him to the inside of the field. Seizing the opportunity, Cody arced toward the left sideline, then, seeing a pack of humanity forming seven yards upfield, he cut back to the inside, nearly losing his footing in the process. He had to reach down with his left hand to keep himself on his feet.

He was running full speed as he crossed the Eagle forty. There was only one defender ahead of him now, and Brett was battling him at the thirty.

Cody tucked the ball in the crook of his right arm, holding on to it as if it were filled with gold. His fingers were spread over the ball's nose, gripping the pebble-grain leather.

Nobody's pryin' this ball from me, Cody thought. *Not even if they bring in the Jaws of Life.*

He felt his legs growing heavy as he crossed the twenty. As he reached the fifteen, he heard the thudding of footsteps behind him. He hoped they belonged to a teammate, but he couldn't risk a look. At the ten, his leg muscles were Jell-O. He tried to lengthen his stride.

At the five, he felt a hand grab his shoulder pads from behind. Then there was another hand on his facemask, jerking him sharply to his right. He tried to strain forward, extending his arms to try to get the ball to break the imaginary plane above the goal line. But, as he would tell Pork Chop later, "It's hard for your body to go one way when your head's going another."

It was Cabrera who dragged Cody down at the two. A face-masking penalty made it first and goal from the one.

"Punch it in, offense! Punch it in, Big O!" Cody heard someone bellow from the stands, as he sat on the bench to get checked out by Dutch and Coach Smith.

"Well, your head's still on your shoulders, right where it's supposed to be," Coach Smith observed. "But how does it feel?"

Tentatively, Cody rolled his neck around, first clockwise, then counterclockwise. "It's fine, Coach," he announced. "I'm glad we do all those neck isometrics in practice."

"That's why we do 'em," Dutch said.

Cody joined Goddard, standing on the sideline. "I wish I were out there, right now," he said. "If I weighed about ten more pounds, I bet I would be on the goal line offense."

"Yeah, Code," Goddard said philosophically, "but look at it this way. If it weren't for you, we wouldn't be down here knockin' on the door in the first place."

After a QB keeper lost half a yard, East's head coach called time out. Cody couldn't hear what he was telling his defensive unit across the field, but his face was as purple as a plum, and he was jumping up and down, as if someone had set him on a hot griddle.

East responded to their coach's histrionics. On second and goal, the Eagles held a team meeting on Berringer's body on an attempted sweep around the right end. On third and goal, Bart was chased out of the pocket and had to fling the ball out of the end zone to avoid taking a sack at the twelve.

"Aw, man," Goddard said, snapping his chin strap, "I was hoping it wouldn't come to this. The pressure's all on me now."

Cody grabbed his shorter, slightly chunky teammate by the shoulders. "You can do this," he urged. "A twenty-yard field goal? You're automatic from there. Just boot it through, man."

The long snap from center was high, but Bart stretched and snagged it, spun the laces away from Goddard, and held the ball perfectly perpendicular to the turf.

Goddard kicked the ball so hard that it sailed through the uprights and didn't touch down until it bounced on the track, twenty yards behind the back of the end zone.

Grant kicked off to begin the fourth quarter. Energized by his field goal, Goddard drilled a low line drive that Cabrera mishandled at the fifteen. He had to go back and retrieve the ball at the five, where Betts and Dylan pounced on him.

"Listen," Pork Chop said in the defensive huddle, "we got these guys in a deep hole, and we ain't lettin' 'em out, understand? Let's stop 'em cold, then watch the offense ram it down their throats!"

The Raiders blitzed on first down and Nottingham had to dump the ball off to Williams in the backfield.

Cody pursued the fullback as he tried to find a lane to run in. He smacked into him before he reached the line of scrimmage and clutched for a handful of jersey. Williams, who Cody guessed outweighed him by thirty pounds, kept his legs churning, but Cody was able to slow his momentum enough so that several of his teammates could jump on his back and finish him off. After only a two-yard gain, Williams went down amid a pile of white helmets and red jerseys.

Nottingham overthrew Landers on second down, and Dylan sniffed out a third down reverse, pushing Cabrera out of bounds after only a five-yard gain.

Berringer fair-caught the ensuing punt at the Grant forty-five, and in the next offensive huddle, Bart Evans spoke with more confidence and authority than Cody had heard all season.

"Time is running out on these guys. If we can score once more—or even mount a long drive—they have no chance. It's time to put 'em away. East undefeated? I don't think so!"

During the change of possession, Coach Smith had called the first down play, an off-tackle to Berringer. But Bart called an audible. "They're going to be expecting a run, so we're gonna hit 'em with three-fifteen X Slant."

Cody recognized the play instantly—a fake hand-off to Berringer, then a pass to Cody Martin, running a delayed slant pattern.

"Code," Bart said earnestly, "give your DB the outside leverage so you can beat him inside."

Cody made eye contact with Bart and nodded.

As the offense lined up, Cody glanced at the clock, which read 6:48. Bart took the snap and backed away from center. Suddenly, an East inside linebacker plunged through the line, and it looked as if Bart would be sacked for at least a seven-yard loss. But, as the 'backer closed in, Bart ducked, and his would-be tackler grabbed nothing but air. Bart rolled to his right, gesturing wildly for a receiver to come back toward the line of scrimmage.

Cody, who had only moments ago released his blocker and started his pass pattern, looked back and saw the QB's peril. He planted his right foot in the soft turf and charged back upfield, reversing the slant he had just run. Brett saw him and launched a high, floating pass in his direction.

Cody leaped for the ball, securing it on his fingertips, and then pulled it down to his body. He turned to run, but was swarmed by a cornerback and a safety. Still, the play was good for fifteen yards.

Not wanting to risk his coach's wrath, Bart stuck to the game plan from that point, calling three straight running plays that moved Grant to the East twenty-five.

"Well," Pork Chop said, plucking a wad of grass from the top of his face mask, "it's Goddard time again."

A forty-two-yard field goal was beyond Goddard's range by at least five yards, but Cody hoped that adrenaline could make up the difference. It did. Goddard's kick traveled at least forty-four yards, but did so two yards wide of the left upright.

The teams traded three-and-outs, and when Grant lined up to punt from its own thirty-five, the game clock read 3:09.

"The way we're playing," Coach Smith announced on the sidelines, "I don't think there's enough time for 'em to score twice."

Coach Smith's words seemed reasonable to Cody, until Cabrera fielded the punt at his thirty-three, shook off a tackler, and raced untouched to the end zone. Cody had to hold himself back from bolting from the sidelines to tackle Cabrera, as he began high-stepping at the fifteen. "Oh, man," he muttered to himself, "this is bad, bad news."

After Nottingham booted the extra point, Grant was able to run a minute and a half off the clock before punting, giving East only 1:32 to salvage its perfect season.

The Eagles began their drive from their own forty-one. Landers picked up thirteen yards on a diving catch over the middle. Cabrera rocketed nine yards around right end. Nottingham turned a mad scramble to escape a blitzing Cody into a seven-yard gain and an all-important first down.

When Williams bulled up the middle for another eleven yards—thanks to an effective double-team block on Pork Chop—the Eagles set up shop at the Grant nineteen.

They're in field-goal range already, Cody thought, shaking his head sadly.

But East wasn't thinking field goal. Nottingham hit Cabrera on a dead run on a slant pattern, and only a shoestring tackle by Dylan kept the Eagle halfback from scoring. Cabrera lunged desperately for the end zone, but came up two yards short.

Cody saw Nottingham sprint up to one of the referees, frantically signaling for a time-out. Then he stared at the clock. Five seconds remained.

As the defense formed a half circle around Coach Smith, Cody surveyed his teammates. Pork Chop's chest heaved beneath his jersey, and sweat ran in rivulets from various locations under his helmet. He was mumbling something to himself, which Cody couldn't decipher.

Blood trickled from Dylan's left nostril, and Bart's jersey was torn at the neck, and his game pants were so mud- and grass-stained that Cody was sure they would have to be retired.

Coach Smith cleared his throat. "That number '1' I wrote on the board in the locker room? I guess now it stands for one play. One play that will define our season. It's up to you eleven guys to determine how we'll all remember that one play."

He paused and studied the eyes of his team. "Anyone got anything to add?"

Pork Chop drew in a deep breath and then extended his hand, palm down, in front of him. "Yeah, I got something to say, Coach," he said. "Let's be a wall. No way do they score on us. Not in our house."

"Okay, then," Coach Smith said with a grim smile, placing his hand on Pork Chop's. "Wall, on three!"

The other players stacked their hands, one on top of another. The cry of "Wall!" was loud enough to drown out the cheerleaders, the crowd, and the pep band. Cody stole a glance into the stands. His dad, Pork Chop's brother and father, Robyn, and Blake stood side by side, holding hands. He waited a moment for his dad's eyes to fall on him. Then he placed his fist over his heart, nodded confidently, and sprinted on to the field to join his teammates.

Cody watched the defensive line dig in. Nottingham moved in behind center. East was in an I formation, with Cabrera lined up directly behind Williams.

Here we go, Cody told himself. *It all comes down to this. Dad's in the stands, and I hope Mom's watching from heaven. Okay, East, whatcha gonna do? Send Cabrera over the top? Or will he be a decoy, while Nottingham tries to bootleg it?*

Cody quickly got his answer. He was wrong on both guesses. Nottingham immediately rolled to his right, coming directly at Cody. Then he pitched the ball to Cabrera, who followed Williams, picking up speed with every stride.

Williams's face was twisted in a snarl as he bore down on Cody. Nottingham peeled off to block Brett, driving him to the inside and out of the play.

Now, with Williams and Cabrera thundering toward him, Cody sensed he was alone. Williams's snarl began to turn to a smile as he braced himself for impact.

Cody didn't like the look of that smile. He showed Williams his displeasure by clubbing hard with his left arm. The blow caught Williams high on his outside shoulder, knocking him off balance. Then Cody moved deftly to the outside, shadowing Cabrera as he tried to sweep into the end zone.

Cabrera must have realized he was running out of field, because he braked and angled his body back to the inside of the field.

Pork Chop was waiting at that particular location. The groan that escaped from Cabrera as Pork Chop slammed him on the one-yard line would make Cody smile every time he thought about it for the next three months.

As he charged toward his best friend to congratulate him, Cody thought, *I wish I were big enough to lift you up off the ground in celebration, Chop. I guess that means I wish I were a forklift.*

Cody took a twenty-minute shower after the victory. He would have extended it to twenty-five minutes if the hot water hadn't run out. Coach Smith had sniffled and stammered through most of his post-game speech, but he was able to rein in his emotions long enough to say, "I've never been prouder of a group of young men in my whole life."

When Mr. Evans came in to collect his twins, he detoured to Cody's locker and said, "Young man, I owe you an apology. My boys tell me you're religious. I don't exactly know what religion you represent, but you represent it well."

"Thank you, sir," Cody said. "But I don't really try to represent any religion—just Jesus."

Outside the locker room, Doug Porter and Robyn both called him "a monster." He wasn't sure whose compliment meant more. It was a close call.

Moments later, with their respective fathers' car engines idling, Pork Chop and Cody stood facing each other in the parking lot.

"So," Cody said, grinning, "way to pancake Cabrera and save the day."

Pork Chop wagged his head from side to side. "You made the play and you know it. You did all the hard work. I just mopped up."

"Hey, Chop," Cody said, before turning to leave, "what were you mumbling about before that last play?"

"I wasn't mumbling, dude, I was praying."

"You? Praying?"

"Yeah. Hey, I may be a wild buck, but I'm no atheist. My people, you know, we're deeply spiritual."

"So what were you praying—that you'd win the game and be a hero?"

"No—that you would."

Cody swallowed hard. "You prayed—for me?"

"Yeah, and guess what? Somebody answered."

"Hey, Chop. Thanks."

"You're welcome. Just don't try to hug me. I've heard about you church people and your hugging."

"Don't worry. I'm not gonna try that. I'll just say thanks for being the best friend in the known universe."

Pork Chop smiled. "I'll just say that, too."

Epilogue
The Fifth Quarter

Cody awoke on Sunday morning to the crisp pops and sizzles of bacon frying. He checked his watch, which read 7:28.

Puzzled, he stutter-stepped his way down the stairs to the kitchen. His dad was humming an aimless tune and carefully grabbing long slices of bacon with a pair of tongs that seemed to Cody much too large and unwieldy for the task at hand.

"Dad," he said softly, "you do know it's Sunday, right?"

His father set down the tongs and smiled. "Of course. Will you get the orange juice out of the fridge, please?"

"Uh, okay."

"Don't look so confused, Cody. You can't have breakfast without orange juice."

"I know, Dad, but it's like, seven-thirty on a Sunday morning, and we haven't had breakfast this early on a Sunday since—well, you know."

Luke Martin moved the plate full of bacon from the counter near the stove to the middle of the kitchen table, next to a platter stacked high with cinnamon-raisin toast. "I know," he said quietly. "But we have to eat breakfast this early if we're going to make early service."

Cody shook his head, as he did when trying to get water out of his ears after a leap off the high dive. "Early service?"

"Yes, Cody. We have to go to early service if we're going to get home in time to watch the Broncos together. You know they're playing at Miami today, and that means pregame broadcast at ten-thirty, kickoff at eleven. Deke Porter is coming over to watch with us, and he'll eat all the snacks I bought if we're not here to monitor him."

Cody sat down at the kitchen table and stared dumbfounded at the empty plate in front of him. "I don't get it. Why?"

"I'll tell you why. Because your youth pastor told me a lot of things during the game—between plays, during time-outs and whatnot. Things I didn't know about my own son. Things that made me proud. Things that I know make your mom proud. And he told me about this, uh, incompleteness that's troubling you. Maybe I can help you with that. Because I feel it too."

Cody plucked a piece of bacon for himself. "So, you mean you're going to start going to church again. Maybe stop working all of the time?"

Cody wasn't sure how to read the sigh that followed.

"I don't know, Code. I have been confused by God, even mad at God these last couple of months. So I don't want to make any promises I can't keep. All I can say is that I'm going to try. Starting today."

"Thanks, Dad."

"You're welcome. Now get to eating. We have a busy morning in front of us. Hymns to sing. Maybe they'll do 'Amazing Grace.' A sermon to hear. And a game to watch. I hope the Broncos cream those Miami—uh, um—"

"Dolphins, Dad. Miami Dolphins."

⬤

The congregation did sing "Amazing Grace" as part of early-service worship. Cody's dad bowed his head and closed his eyes, rocking slowly back and forth in rhythm with the melody that brought his wife comfort, even as cancer invaded her body.

Pastor Taylor spoke about the journey of life and how so many people "are obsessed with where they are going, how soon they are going to get there, and how many riches they can accumulate along the way."

"I feel sorry for those people," the pastor said. "They are missing something so very key. You see, my friends, life isn't merely about where you are going and all of that. It's more about who you have beside you—and who you have living in your heart—on the way."

Cody's dad put his arm around him and drew him close when he heard those words. Then they stood together for prayer. As soon as Pastor Taylor said, "Amen," Cody dashed to the foyer. There he selected the largest of the premium early-service donuts—a jelly-filled monstrosity smothered with thick chocolate icing and crowned with red, white, and blue sprinkles.

"Man," he whispered as he carefully placed the pastry on a napkin and headed for the exit, "this baby's almost as big as a football. Chop's gonna love it!"

SPIRIT
OF THE
GAME

Will Cody
survive
the cut?

FULL-COURT PRESS

BY TODD HAFER

Zonder**kidz**

Chapter 1
Trial and Air

I t's time to attempt suicide!"
barked Coach Clayton.

"Everyone on the line!"

"Aww—I hate suicides," Alston groaned. Cody
looked at the star point guard, who was bent over
beside him, hands on his knees. Terry Alston's neck
gleamed with perspiration. The back of his sweat-
soaked gray practice T-shirt clung tightly to his back.
Cody studied the sweat stain, noting that its shape
looked like the continent of Africa.

"Here's the deal," Coach Clayton said with a smile.
"Whoever wins the first suicide gets to shower. The
rest of you—ah, I pity the rest of you. Because I'm

going to work you like government mules. Now, let's see who's quick enough to escape the pain."

"The first day of tryouts wasn't like this last year," Alston whispered. "This new coach—I don't like him."

"I heard he coached at Holmes last year." said Pork Chop, who, sitting to Cody's left, was frantically lacing up a size-ten Nike. "I saw him shooting before practice. He's got game."

"Whatever," Alston snorted. "And don't worry about your shoelaces, Chop. You're not gonna win this suicide anyway. It takes you too long to get all of that beef moving."

"You never know," Pork Chop replied, smiling grimly. "When I get all this beef moving, the momentum is something to behold. I might win. Even Cody here might take it. At least neither of us smokes Marlboros, like you do."

Alston arched his eyebrows. "Martin? Win? He's got no wheels. Do you, Martin?"

Cody stared at his worn-out Adidas. He felt anger rising inside him. Then he thought of the words his youth pastor, Blake Randall, spoke on Sunday— "When words are many, sin is not absent."

Cody felt too tired to say anything sinful, but he decided it was best to take no chances. He stared straight ahead and stayed silent.

Pork Chop finished double-lacing his shoe and rose slowly to his feet.

"Well," said Pork Chop, "they say this Colorado air is thinner than in other places. That ought to give us nonsmokers an edge."

Instantly, Coach Clayton blew a shrill blast on his whistle. Alston swore under his breath and exploded off the baseline at the south end of the court.

Alston had the fastest feet Cody had ever seen. He touched the near free throw line with his left foot, then changed direction like a ricochet. He reached the south end line again—two strides ahead of Cody— then sprinted for half court. Cody struggled to keep up. He stayed low, he ran straight, and he didn't look around. He focused on each line. The squeaking shoes, panting, and occasional swearing swirled around him in another dimension.

He wasn't gaining any ground on Alston, but he wasn't losing any either. On the long last sprint, from end line to end line, Alston slowed noticeably. *Must be the cigarettes*, Cody thought. He pumped his arms furiously and focused on driving his knees forward. As he crossed half court, he was only a step behind Alston. Cody lengthened his stride, straining to devour the distance between himself and the fastest athlete in the school.

As they hit the south free throw line, Cody saw Alston glance over his shoulder. They were almost stride for stride now. As they crossed the end line, Alston's track experience saved him. He leaned forward, edging Cody by inches. Victorious, Alston slammed into the slice of crimson wrestling mat that hung on the wall under the basket. Then he slumped to the floor and coughed like a barking seal.

Cody kicked the wall in disgust. Pork Chop finished third, two strides behind Cody. He sunk to his hands and knees, his caramel skin wet with sweat, and began panting as if he were trying to blow out birthday candles—lots of them.

Meanwhile, Alston had staggered to the gym's south doors. He stood under the green exit sign, smiling. "Have a nice run, boys!" he laughed before erupting into another coughing fit.

Coach Clayton glared at Alston. "I suggest you shut up, Slick. Save your air. And I suggest you learn to do without the cigarettes this season. I don't allow 'em."

Alston gave the coach a startled look, then exited the gym as if it were on fire.

Pork Chop shook his head. "Man, how does Coach know Alston smokes? Does he have ESP or something?"

"How many eighth graders cough like coal miners?" Cody asked.

"Alston's been smoking since he was twelve," noted Brett Evans, the better of the Evans twins—although both had made the starting five the previous season.

"It's not fair that he won," Bart Evans said. "He cheats. He never touches all the lines!"

Coach Clayton's whistle pierced Cody's eardrums again. As he planted his foot on the free throw line, he felt a blister forming on his right instep. He tried to keep his weight on the outside of his foot, but then his calf started to cramp. He finished suicide number two just behind Brett. Pork Chop was third again.

Midway through the third suicide, Cody felt the chili-dog and thirty-two-ounce soda he had for lunch rising in his throat. He finished running, dropping to fourth place this time, then dashed from the gym, through the small foyer between the gym and the locker room. Once outside, he doubled over and relinquished his lunch on a knee-high pile of snow that had been cleared from the entryway at the school's south end.

He straightened and watched his breath vaporize in front of his face as he exhaled heavily. His throat burned, and his stomach muscles ached, as if he had been gut-punched. He turned and jogged back to the gym.

Coach Clayton smiled as Cody toed the line again. "Lose your lunch, Martin?"

"Oh, I bet he didn't lose it, Coach," Pork Chop said. "I bet he knows right where it is."

Cody thought he was too spent to smile, but he felt an almost involuntary tugging at the corners of his mouth.

"I'll tell you what," Coach Clayton said, "if you all will make this one count—really bust it—we're done, okay? But if I see even one guy dogging it, you'll keep running. I don't care if we go all night."

Cody inhaled hungrily. "One more," he said quietly to no one in particular. He heard the whistle and willed his feet to move. He concentrated on braking with his left foot. He knew he had opened the blister on his right and guessed it was the size of a quarter at least.

ISBN 0-310-70668-8

Available now at your local bookstore!

Zonder**kidz**

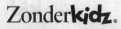

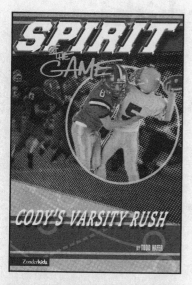
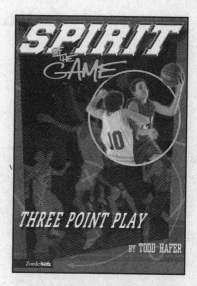

We want to hear from you. Please send your comments about this
book to us in care of zreview@zondervan.com. Thank you.

Zonder**kidz**.

Grand Rapids, MI 49530
www.zonderkidz.com